Please feel free to send me an email ᵀ my
publisher filters these ⌐ velcome.

Alexandria Ayeı

Sign up for my blc ᵤₛᵢ
http://alexayers.org

About the Publisher

BLVNP Incorporated, A Nevada Corporation, 340 S. Lemon #6200, Walnut CA 91789, info@blvnp.com / legal@blvnp.com

DISCLAIMER

Praise for Psycho Sitter

This book was so good, when I heard it was getting published I was so happy! This is probably the only book I've ever read in a matter of one day. The plot and the story line flow amazingly, couldn't have done a better job! Must read!

-gaby, Amazon

Most thrilling book that I have ever read! I have already bought the book and read it twice, that's how amazing this book is. I give major props to the author Alexandria Ayers for writing such a captivating story, especially at such a young age. Great job.

-Darlene boltz, Amazon

I absolutely loved this book. My daughter told me about it and I'm so glad I checked it out. Once I started reading it, I couldn't put it down till I was finished, and then I wanted more!! I'm so glad it's getting published!

-S. Dzurick, Amazon

I really love this book, I started reading it on wattpad before I new it was getting published. When I heard i wasn't surprised because of how amazingly well it was written and was really happy. But I very highly recommend you read this it is one of my all time favorites.

-Caitlin Sexton, Goodreads

This is one of my favorite books and I'm proud to have been with it since the start. You're amazing and a genius Alexandria :)

-Megan, Goodreads

Psycho Sitter

By: Alexandria Ayers

BLVNP

ISBN: 978-1-68030-847-1

Table of contents

PROLOGUE 1

CHAPTER 1 6

CHAPTER 2 12

CHAPTER 3 16

CHAPTER 4 20

CHAPTER 5 23

CHAPTER 6 27

CHAPTER 7 30

CHAPTER 8 34

CHAPTER 9 38

CHAPTER 10 43

CHAPTER 11 46

CHAPTER 12 50

CHAPTER 13 54

CHAPTER 14 57

CHAPTER 15 60

CHAPTER 16 63

CHAPTER 17 67

CHAPTER 18 71

CHAPTER 19 75

CHAPTER 20 78

CHAPTER 21 83

CHAPTER 22 86

CHAPTER 23 91

CHAPTER 24 95

CHAPTER 25 98

CHAPTER 26 102

CHAPTER 27 106

CHAPTER 28 112

CHAPTER 29 115

CHAPTER 30 124

CHAPTER 31 132

CHAPTER 32 137

CHAPTER 33 145

CHAPTER 34 149

CHAPTER 35 155

CHAPTER 36 160

CHAPTER 37 164

CHAPTER 38 169

CHAPTER 39 171

CHAPTER 40 174

CHAPTER 41 178

CHAPTER 42 183

CHAPTER 43 188

CHAPTER 44 193

CHAPTER 45 197

CHAPTER 46 202

CHAPTER 47 205

CHAPTER 48 208

CHAPTER 49 212

CHAPTER 50 217

EPILOGUE 229

FREE DOWNLOAD

Get these freebies and MORE when you sign up for the author's mailing list!

http://alexayers.org/

Prologue

I started tapping my fingertips on the steering wheel as I waited outside her house. Her parents should be leaving soon, so it wouldn't be too long now. I tried to focus on planning what I was going to do, but all that seemed to fill my mind was how stupid the young girl's parents are. Hiring a sitter online isn't always dangerous, but if you're ignorant enough not to check the reviews on the website, and at least ask for background checks, then you're asking for trouble.

As far as her mother and father knew, they were waiting for Susan Kelly, a forty-six-year-old woman and a loving and caring mother of four, with a degree in nursing and only three speeding tickets on her record. But little did they know that a storm had headed their way. Of course, that storm was devilishly handsome and is known as me. Who else would it be?

"How much longer do you think it'll be before they leave?" Lane asked, resting his head on the steering wheel. His car was parked only a few feet away from mine.

"Shouldn't be too much longer," I replied, glancing over at the house. We had to park behind a bundle of trees on the other side of a small field that's between us and the house. I swear, these people live in the middle of nowhere. If anything were to happen, they would be screwed — plain and simple. Why would they even want to live in the country, anyway? There's nothing to do, and on top of that, it smells like shit. Hell, I wouldn't be surprised if we were smelling actual shit.

"I'm hungry. Can we come back later? Or how about we just skip out on this one? I'm tired." Lane groaned.

"If you're really that hungry and tired, then leave, because there's no way I'm skipping out on this one. Phil would have my head if he knew I didn't bring one back. I need to keep up with my reputation." I glanced at him with annoyance. It's tiring having to explain this to him — especially since I've told him only about a million times already.

Phil was our boss, and I knew the moment he handed me her file, I needed to have her. I had to be the one to bring her in. She was mine from the moment my eyes saw her bright, forest green ones.

"Fine. You have fun. I'm getting something to eat then head back to the field."

After Lane left, my thoughts started to drift on how she would react. Would she come willingly? Fight me and threaten to kill me? Or would she be just confused and almost unsure on how to react? I've seen all of them. Tears, rage, unsureness. It's always those three. I'd learned that much over the years of being in this... well you can call it a "unique" business.

Some people say this job is sick or twisted. Sometimes they'd ask, "Why would you want to work there, you sick freak?"

But they don't know that feeling I get when I see the fear and confusion written on the features of the unlikely young girls, who happened to fall into the trap of sex trafficking, or what we like to call pleasuring; the rich likes to call it shopping.

For the customers, it truly is just like going in the store and buying a toy. You pick the one you fancy, and after that, you pay. There's a catch, though. With this job, you get to keep the merchandise for only one night. Also, you can't keep the baby dolls. They're far too precious. That's what I tell the people who don't understand my job.

I saw movement in the house. It looked like the parents were leaving. I could just make out, what I assume, was the mother embracing her children then letting go just a bit too soon because of her husband pulling her away. This would be the last time she would hold her children in her arms. It's a shame they didn't hug longer.

As they got into their car, they sped down the old country road. I'm guessing they're running late for their flight.

Instead of driving up towards the home and barging inside, I decided that I'd wait for a while and let the thought of their sitter no longer coming to linger around.

Lane had probably made it back by now and, most likely, stuffed his face with only God knows what. I wonder if he'd be flying back to London tonight. I kind of hope he does, so he'd be out of my way. Plus, I didn't want him coming back here and trying to help me bring her in. She's mine, not his. I called the shots.

At first I saw her eyes, then I saw her. Her picture in the school yearbook, which Phil gave me, told me a lot about her appearance. She's beautiful. I have to say, she'll sell great, meaning an even bigger check for me. Gorgeous, more money. Double hit. Lucky me.

3

The only thing that is so annoying about her is that her brother is with her. I was still debating on what I could do to the little brat. Maybe I should just leave him here? No, he'd just call the cops and get my ass hauled to jail, even though he's only a kid. I'm already in enough trouble. If the Feds find out about this job, I'll be locked up for, no telling, how many years.

I'll have to think of something because I can't take the dipshit with me. I'm afraid to even think of what Phil would do if I brought in a boy. He'll probably think I'm nuts and cut my check. There's no way I'd let him do that. I work too hard not to get paid less than what I already do. Anyway, he knows that he shouldn't mess with me. I bring in most of the girls, so he can't do a thing to me unless he wants to lose his best employee.

After sitting in the car for a few more hours, I couldn't stand it anymore. I needed to go and get her. I opened the SUV door, jumped out, and headed towards the home. After making sure I had my gun and pocket knife in my jacket, I exited the vehicle. The crisp January air pierced through my thin clothes as I treaded on the snow-blanketed ground.

Before I reached the entrance, I noticed that all the lights in the house seemed to be turned off. Maybe they knew I was coming? No, that's not possible. It's pitch black out here, there's no way they could have seen me.

I shrugged it off and headed for the front door. After knocking three times, I pulled out a cigarette, placed the hazardous paper stick between my lips, and leaned on the door frame. A minute passed before a young boy opened the door, fear written all over his face.

"Hello," I spoke, looking down at the boy.

Seconds later, she appeared.

I was met with long, unruly hair and bright, green eyes, staring at me suspiciously. The picture in that file really did her no justice. A slender figure with slim torso and compelling legs. There's no denying it — she's hot as hell. It's been a long time since I've seen someone with a body like hers.

She shielded her brother. She placed herself in front of him as she watched me light a second cigarette. I brought it to my lips and breathed out the smoke. I wonder if the reason that she's looking at me with a worried face—which still looks hot—had something to do with the fact that I looked like a psychopathic murderer, or she could somehow see the money signs on my eyes.

"Who are you and what do you want?" Her mellifluous voice echoed across the empty fields.

It hadn't been that long yet, but I was already intrigued.

Chapter 1

Cassandra

I was walking down the halls of Britwood High School with my best friend Summer. As I opened the door to the parking lot, the cool January air hit my face, making a shiver run down my back. The ground was covered with a blanket of snow, making it look like a winter wonderland.

"Are you listening to me?" Summer's voice broke my thoughts.

"W-what? Oh, um..." I stuttered.

"I asked, what you're doing later. I thought maybe we could hang out."

"I told you earlier, my parents are leaving for Australia tonight, and the sitter is coming, so I can't have friends over," I said.

"Oh yeah. But I can come over later this week, right?" she asked, opening her car door.

"Well my parents said no friends over this week because I'm in trouble," I said, looking down at the ground.

"What'd you get into trouble for?"

"For not picking up Ben from school. He was left standing outside the school when it was below freezing," I said, looking down, ashamed.

Summer started laughing and clapping her hands.

"You forgot your own brother when it was below freezing?"

"Yeah..."

"Is that why you have to have a sitter?" she asked, finally able to control her laughter.

"Yeah, they said if I couldn't even remember to pick up my own brother from school, then there was no way they were leaving him with me for a week."

"Well I wouldn't either," Summer said, getting in her car.

"Bye! See ya later." she shouted before closing her door.

I yelled a bye back then got in my piece of junk, my truck, and pulled out of the school parking lot.

* * *

I got out of my truck and headed for the front door.

"I'm home!" I yelled from the door, kicking off my shoes and taking off my coat.

"I'm in here!" I heard my mother's voice call from the kitchen.

I walked into the kitchen, where I saw my mother preparing some kind of soup.

"I'm making you, Ben, and the sitter some potato soup," she said, stirring the so called "soup."

My mother was never a very good cook, but then again, neither was I.

"Speaking of the sitter, when will she be here?" I asked, stepping towards the gross-looking, chunky liquid.

"In about thirty minutes." I looked up at the clock above the sink to see that it was 5:30 pm.

"Well I better be getting my suitcase in the car," my mother said, and she headed upstairs.

I decided just to watch some TV.

* * *

"Now make sure to use your manners, do whatever she says, and be nice," my mother said.

I just rolled my eyes, I already knew to do that. I don't know why she had to tell us.

"Okay, I love you," she said, giving my little brother, Ben, a huge hug then gave me one.

I didn't really hug back, I was still mad at her for not trusting me with Ben. Yes, I know I forgot about picking him, but I didn't mean to. She just doesn't have faith in me.

"I love you, guys. The sitter should be here in a few minutes. You think you can handle Ben?" Mom asked, looking straight at me.

"Yes, mom, I'm pretty sure I can handle him for a few minutes," I said, annoyed.

"We love you, and we'll see you two in a week," Dad said, trying to get my mother to leave before they missed their plane.

"Bye, love you." Mom said as Dad shut the front door.

I turned around to look at Ben and said, "What do you wanna do, brat?"

"I'm hungry, poophead." Ben has been calling me that for years. He says it's because my hair color looks a lot like "poop".

"There's soup on the stove," I said, going to the kitchen.

"Did mom cook it?" He sounded kinda worried because he knew mom couldn't cook.

"Yeah, she did." I said, smiling, as I opened the door of the fridge, got out some leftover pizza, and put it on a plate.

"Please," Ben said, looking up at me with puppy dog eyes.

"Please what?" I spat, looking down at the blond-haired boy.

"Share. I don't want to eat mom's chunky soup,'" he said, looking at the two slices of pizza on the paper plate.

"No way," I said, walking to the living room.

"Please, Cassie."

He said, grabbing my arm. I looked down at him only to see tears in his blues eyes. Great, I made him cry.

"Fine." I gave him a slice.

"Yes!" He took the piece, ran, and jumped on the couch. "That little rat," I thought.

We watched TV for a couple of hours until we noticed it was already eight o'clock. I was wondering if that sitter was even coming. Maybe she got lost or something. It was dark outside, and sometimes it could be hard to see the road signs. Just then the TV shut off, along with the lights, leaving us sitting in the dark.

"Cass, what's going on?" Ben said, hugging onto my side.

"I don't know—" A knock on the door made me and Ben both jump back.

"Don't move," I said slowly. The knock on the door got louder.

"Maybe it's the sitter," Ben said, still holding onto me for dear life. He hates the dark. He'll do anything not to be in the dark.

"Maybe," I said.

"Maybe they can turn the lights back on," he said and ran towards the door.

"No Ben!" I yelled, running after him.

It was too late, though, he had already unlocked and opened the door.

"Hello," a deep raspy voice said.

I grabbed Ben and put him behind me. The only thing I could really see about the man standing in front of me was that he was tall and had a cigarette between his lips. I squinted, trying to see more of him. He put his hand in one of his pockets as he pulled out an object. I didn't know what it was till he moved his finger down on it, making a small flame ignite out of the silver hole.

I could now see his face. He had brown, curly hair that was swiped over to one side, an eyebrow ring, and a lip ring. He had tattoos running up on his neck, but that's not what caught my attention the most. It was his piercing green eyes. They were so beautiful and captivating.

"Take a picture. It'll last longer, babe." His deep voice snapped me out of my thoughts.

He walked past me and into the house, looking around like he was trying to find something, even though he could barely see anything because the lights were out.

"What are you doing?" I spoke for the first time since he showed up.

"Looking for the basement." I stopped in my tracks. Why would he want to know where the basement was?

"W-why?" I stuttered, scared of the answer.

"To tie you up and put you down there."

Chapter 2

I froze as the words left his lips, leaving me and Ben standing there scared to death.

I heard a raspy laugh come from the man's mouth. He turned around with a smirk plastered on his face as he said, "I'm messing with you… Maybe." He said the last part so quietly that I barely heard it.

Ben was now attached to my arm, not daring to let go. The man then looked at Ben, smiling.

"Take me to the basement, kid." His voice rang in the silent house.

I looked down at Ben to see him shaking his head "no."

"Well you're going to anyway," he said and grabbed Ben's small arm, starting to pull him away from me.

I stood there frozen, knowing I had to do something.

"No!" I yelled out.

The man stopped dead in his tracks and looked at me.

"I-I'll take y-you," I stuttered, walking over to Ben and grabbing his arm from the man's grasp while whispering in his ear. "Call the cops once we're out of sight.'" Ben nodded.

The man grabbed my arm and pulled me away from my little brother. I led him into the kitchen where the basement door was. I opened the door to the basement and looked down at the dark hole. I always hated going in our basement because it wasn't like any of my friend's basements. Theirs were finished and turned into game rooms, while mine was just a storage area with very little light and concrete walls and floor.

"Ladies first," he said, looking down at the basement door.

I decided not to argue with him and just went down first. As I was walking down the steps, I could feel him coming closer till he's just one step behind me.

I stopped in my tracks as his breathe fanned my bare neck. He whispered in my ear, "I heard what you told your brother." His raspy voice rang in my ear. "And you're going to pay for it." He finished.

Not being able to move from pure fear, I froze on the spot.

"Move!" He yelled and pushed me about three steps down.

I lost my balance and plummeted face first on the stairs. I shielded my head with my arms, ready for the impact, but it never came. I opened my eyes to see that my face was only inches from one of the wooden steps. I felt strong arms wrap around my waist. I looked over my shoulder to see that the man had caught me. He pulled me up and set me back on my feet.

"Thank you." I whispered and continued to walk till we're now on the ground level.

"Where's your box at?" he asked.

"What box?" I asked, raising one eyebrow.

"The electrical box," he said.

I felt pretty dumb. I mean, what else could he be down here for? I took him to where the box was. He opened the lid and pushed a few buttons. Minutes later, the lights came back on, making it a little less scary. I took this time to observe him while he was still messing around with the electrical box. I could now see one of his tattoos on his collarbone very well. It was very small, compared to the rest of those that run up on his neck. It was written

in fine cursive. The two simple words didn't really strike me as a tattoo that he would get. "I'm sorry," it said. I wonder what he's sorry for.

I snapped out of my thoughts when his deep voice spoke.

"W-what?" I stuttered.

"I said, move." I didn't think twice before moving out of his way.

He walked past me and jogged upstairs. I almost had to run to keep up with his long strides.

Once back in the kitchen, I was hoping and praying that Ben called the cops but I didn't see or hear sirens.

I walked into the living room to see Ben sitting on the couch. I mouthed to him, "Did you call the cops?" He shook his head "no." I walked over to him and sat down and asked him, "Why?"

"I couldn't. The house phone wouldn't work, and I couldn't find your cellphone," he said and looked down.

"Cassie, what's going to happen to us?" Just as he said that, the man came back and stood before us with an angry expression.

"Heard someone was going to call the cops. Is that true?" His piercing green eyes locked with my little brother's. Ben just sat there and shook his head even though the man already knew he was going to.

"Don't lie to me!" the man said and raised his hand to slap Ben.

"No!" I said.

He stopped his hand mid-air and looked at me.

"No, i-it w-was my f-fault," I said and looked up at the man.

"Well in that case," he yelled and slapped me across the face.

My head snapped back at the impact. His slap left my right cheek stinging. I looked up through my hair to see a confused man standing in front of me. A tear slipped out of my eye and ran down my cheek. The man stomped into to the kitchen and started screaming random cuss words. Then I heard what sounded like glass shattering.

"Cassie," Ben's voice said.

I turned my head to look at him and saw worry written all over his face. A small tear fell from his left eye. I wiped it away before it could fall. I brought his small body onto my lap and held him close.

"What's going to happen to us?" he asked.

"I-I don't know." I truly didn't know.

All that I knew was that the man in the kitchen was a psycho.

Chapter 3

It's been about an hour since the man had slapped me and gone into the kitchen. In that past hour, all I've heard was glass being thrown and shattered. I still let Ben rest on my lap. I looked down to see my little brother asleep in my arms.

I looked over to the clock sitting on top of the fireplace, it read 11:46 pm. Just then, I heard the man come back into the living room. My hands started to sweat and shake. They always do when I'm scared or nervous. I looked down again at Ben, pulling him closer to me.

"Get up," he said, annoyed.

I did what he said and got up, heading for the stairs.

"Oh yeah, there's a mess in the kitchen. You can clean up." I let out a groan and continued walking up the stairs.

Once in the hall way, I headed for the first door on the left, opened it, and set Ben down on his twin-sized bed. I pulled the duvet over his chest, kissed his forehead, and then headed back down the steps. Even though Ben might get on my nerves sometimes, deep down I still loved him.

Back in the living room, I saw the man sitting on the couch and messing with his phone. I somehow gained enough courage to walk over to him.

"What's your name and why are you here?" I blurted out.

He looked up from his phone and said, "That's none of your business," he snapped at me.

"Well at least tell me your name," I asked, hoping to get something out of him.

"Hunter," his deep voice rang.

"Now go clean up the kitchen." He smirked and looked at his phone.

"No." The word slipped out before I knew I said it. He looked at me with a shocked expression.

"What?" He growled and stood up.

I took a step back but still held my ground. His height towered over me. I looked him straight in the eyes and said no with all my courage. The thing that happened next shocked me. He slapped me on the face, sending me to the ground, holding my right cheek. I felt the tears coming. I tried to hold them back, not wanting him to see me as weak; but one slipped out anyway.

He got down to my level and said, "No will never be an answer for me." And with that, he got up and went off somewhere.

I lay there for a few minutes, just letting the tears fall and not knowing what was going to happen to me and my brother. It scared me more than anything.

Once the tears dried up, and there were no more left to fall, I got up and went to the kitchen to find pieces of glass scattered everywhere. I walked over to the basement door where the broom stood in the corner. I grabbed it and started sweeping the small pieces of glass, being careful not to step on any. I started to think back to when Hunter told me his name. His name just doesn't really fit someone like him. It sounds so much… It just doesn't sound like a name he would have. It just doesn't fit him. I continued to sweep the pieces, letting the thought of Hunter's name driftl to the back of my mind, not wanting to think about the man who just hit me.

After I finished sweeping the floor, I walked over to put the broom back when I felt something stab my foot. I let out a scream of pain and sat down on the floor tiles, holding my foot. Tears started to fall as I saw blood pouring out of the cut. I heard what sounded like someone running down the steps, then Hunter came jogging into the kitchen with a worried look. I looked away from him, knowing he didn't care about me. I directed my attention back to my bleeding foot. I heard him walk closer. I just held my foot closer to me till I felt two cold, strong arms wrap around my back and under my legs. Carrying me, Hunter walked up the stairs and towards the bathroom.

"Put me down," I said, trying to get away from his grasp. "Shut up," he said and continued to walk up the stairs.

Once we got to the bathroom, he set me down on the counter and shut the door with his foot.

"How did you have this?" He asked while looking at my bleeding foot.

"I stepped on the glass that you broke," I said, annoyed, and looked away from him.

"If you had never gotten mad—".

"So now it's my fault?" He yelled.

"Yes, it is your fault!" I snapped back, my temper getting the best of me.

"You know what? J-just shut up!" He yelled and grabbed my foot, making me wince in pain.

Hunter put one of his hands in his pocket, dug around till he found what he needed, then pulled it out. My heart stopped. He held a black pocket knife.

Chapter 4

I sat there on the bathroom counter, staring at the black shiny object in Hunter's hands. I was not able to concentrate on anything else in the room except the black pocket knife he held in his large hands. I began to shake. My hands then started to get wet. I was afraid of what could possibly happen next. Probably sensing my uneasiness, Hunter looked up at me. We made eye contact for maybe two seconds before I looked away, afraid of his intentions with the knife.

"Afraid, babe?" His raspy voice broke the fidgeting of my hands.

Instead of saying anything, I just sat there, trying to think of something other than the possible chance of me dying at this moment in the hallway bathroom.

From the corner of my eye, I could see Hunter crouching down to inspect my bleeding foot. Not wanting to see what would happen, I closed my eyes as I felt something sharp pierce into my flesh. I quickly grabbed onto the closest thing I could find. I ended up gripping the bathroom counter. And squeezing my eyes shut tightly, he continuously pierced the fairly long pocket knife into my sensitive foot.

Minutes had already passed, but Hunter still tried to get the piece of glass out of the bottom of my foot. I let out a muffled scream when Hunter pushed the knife too hard. A tear fell and ran down my right cheek. I opened my eyes as Hunter pushed the knife harder. I looked down at the head of curls before me. I tried to pull away from him, but he just grabbed my foot again and forced the sharp tip of the pocket knife back into my now bloody foot.

"Y-you're h-hurting m-me." I croaked in between cries. He still didn't listen. He just forced the sharp object harder. "Hunter!" I finally yelled.

He quickly looked up at me. Instead of the piercing green eyes, I was met with dark, green pools. I quickly pulled my foot closer towards me, and knew then that something wasn't right about him. I mean, yes, I already knew that something was missing, but right then he just looked like a plain psycho.

"D-don't hurt me. Please," I cried.

In seconds, his eyes changed back to their normal color. Then he just jolted up from his position and stormed out, leaving me sitting there, clueless of what's going on. I looked down at my foot to see blood still coming out of the small cut right above my heel. Still shocked from Hunter's behavior, I got off the counter. I opened the cabinet below the sink and looked for a bandage of some sort. After I dug around, I finally found what I was looking for. I took the bandage and wrapped it around my foot.

Once done, I tiptoed out of the bathroom and headed to my room, hoping I would not to get caught by Hunter. As I entered, I heard a scream of pain from downstairs. I quickly ran down, not really thinking about what could be going on. I just wanted to know why there was screaming.

When I was downstairs, I heard heavy breathing coming from the kitchen. I hurried and ran towards the room, only to be met with a pacing and frightened Hunter. He grabbed his curls and continued to scream words that I couldn't quite make out.

"Hunter," I said slowly while I approached him.

He looked at me with puffy bloodshot eyes.

"I did it! I was the one!" He screamed half to me, half to himself.

"What? What, Hunter?" I slowly said, not to scare him.

"I...I k-killed them..." When the words left his lips, I felt my heart drop.

"I-I can get y-you h-help, Hunter. I can," I said calmly, so that I won't trigger anything. But what resulted was something completely opposite.

"No! I'm sick and tired of people telling me I need help!" I didn't even have time to comprehend what was said before his fist hit my head and I felt my body hit the ground with a thud.

My eyes started to close slowly. The last thing I remembered was slowly fading into a world of darkness.

Chapter 5

"Cassie." I heard a small voice called my name.

I tried to open my eyes but I just couldn't seem to get them to.

"Cassie, you have to wake up. You can't leave me here by myself with that man," the voice cried.

I slowly realized to whom the voice belonged. It was Ben's.

"Please, don't leave me. I never meant the mean things I said. I love you, Cassandra, a lot" His voice continued to cry over my body.

I again tried my hardest to open my eyes, and this time they did.

"I love you too, Ben." I quietly said to the crying boy in front of me.

His eyes opened as soon as he heard my voice.

"Cassie!" He mused and hugged me as tight as he could.

"I thought you died, and… A-and I'm so glad you're alright!" he said and hugged me again.

After our sister-brother moment, I asked the young boy in front of me a question. "Where's Hunter?" Ben looked at me with funny expression. "The man, where's the man?"

"Oh, the man. Yeah, he went down to the basement," Ben said.

"What is he doing down there?" I asked, wondering why he would go back down there.

"He said he just needed to cool off and for me to keep an eye on you," he said while helping me sit up.

I nodded and asked, "How long have I been out?"

"Well this morning, I went to your room but you weren't there so I came down here to find that man sitting beside you on the floor. He looked in pain so I really don't know." He breathed out.

"Well he knocked me out last night." I said looking down.

"He knocked you out?" Ben raised his voice.

"Yes. Now, how long has he been down in the basement?" I asked.

"He went down there like, maybe, uh, like five minutes ago or something." I stumbled a little, trying to get off the kitchen tiles and then stood upright.

"What are you doing?" Ben asked, grabbing onto my arm while I walked over to the basement door.

I turned around to face him and said, "We're getting out of here," I said, smiling at my little brother. Soon his smile matched mine.

"Now go upstairs but be quiet and grab my backpack and get your shoes and coat on," I ordered.

He nodded then quietly hurried up the stairs. While he went upstairs to get his things, I went over to the basement door and looked down, making sure Hunter was nowhere in sight. Having not seen him, I quietly shut the door and locked it. It was followed by hooking the latch. But I still needed something else to put in front of the door so I looked around the room, and my eyes fell on this cabinet that holds Mom's nice dishes. I quickly ran over to it and slowly tried to push it towards the door. After a good three minutes of pushing and tugging on the oversized cabinet, it was finally in front of the basement door.

"I got the stuff, Cassie," Ben said, coming back into the kitchen.

"Okay good. Now go grab my shoes there in front of the door in the living room and get my coat please." With that, he handed my backpack to me and was off to get my things.

I ran over to the fridge and grabbed five bottles of water then ran over to the cabinets and stuffed some protein bars in the backpack and then threw in some other snacks.

"Here are your shoes and coat," Ben said, handing me my things.

"Thanks." I quickly put on my boots and laced them up, moved onto my coat and buttoned it, and put the backpack on my shoulders.

"Come on, Ben, let's get out of here," I said as I grabbed onto his arm, walked over to the back door, opened it, and then shut it behind us.

"Why are we going this way?" he asked. "I'll explain in a little bit. We just need to get out of sight first." He nodded then followed me down the back steps.

All we have to do is cross the field then get into the woods to be out of sight.

I still couldn't believe Hunter punched me and knocked me out. There's something seriously wrong with that man, but I guess one good thing is that he got the piece of glass out of my foot. It still hurt like hell every time I take a step, though. I wasn't limping too badly so I could still run, though not just as fast as I could if my foot wasn't hurt.

We hurried and went into the forest of trees, trying to get out of sight. But before we completely got into the forest, I looked back only to find Hunter standing on the back porch of the house, holding what looks like a gun.

Chapter 6

We have a choice in this world: to give up when life gets tough or fight for what we believe in.

Many of us do the first. We give up when things get hard. Most of us don't even try to overcome the problems we face. We simply say things like *there's no point I'll lose anyways* or *what's the point of trying when there's no hope.* We all want to win. We just don't want to fight because we feel as if there's no hope. But I'm not like that.

I believe in hope and fighting for what you love. The man standing on the porch with a gun pointed right at me and my younger brother needs to know that I'm not giving up.

"Run," I said, not looking away from the hard stare of the man standing on the back porch.

"What?"

"I said, run Ben." I turned to look at him.

"Trust me." With that, my younger brother took off and run into the forest, leaving me standing there and smirking at Hunter.

I raised my right hand in the air and slowly put down every finger except the middle one. Then I took off running in the woods.

I could see Ben about thirty yards ahead of me. I knew he was a slow runner that's why I let him go ahead of me. When I heard the sound of Hunter's gun going off, I looked behind me only to see him still on the porch, shooting the gun in mid-air.

"Game on, Cassandra!" His deep voice boomed throughout the forest and the field.

I made the mistake of looking behind me again. I now saw him off the porch and running through the field towards us. I ran as fast as my short legs would go, trying to catch up with Ben. It was even harder to run when you have a backpack filled with bottles of water and a foot that was just cut last night due to a glass that was stuck in it.

"Keep running, buddy," I said to Ben as I was only five feet behind him.

"Is he chasing us?" he asked out of breath.

"Yes, but it will be okay. I promise," I reassured him. I was now running beside him.

* * *

We'd been running non-stop for probably twenty minutes, trying to make some distance between us and Hunter. I think it's working because he's now out of sight.

In a little bit, my asthma had really been acting up. I'd tried to not let it bother me but it's kinda hard when your chest feels really tight and your breathing isn't normal.

"Can we stop for a few minutes, Cassie? I'm really tired," Ben's little out-of-breath voice spoke.

"Yeah, we can. I'm tired too, buddy," I admitted, slowing down and stopping by a tree. I took off my backpack, let it sit by the tree, and then sit down leaning against the trunk.

Ben sat beside me, leaning his hand on my shoulder.

"Can you give me a water please?" he asked, looking at the backpack.

"Yeah," I said, unzipping the pack, getting out two waters, and handing one to him.

After drinking half of the water in the bottle, Ben was asleep. His head was now in my lap. I grabbed the blanket, packed it, and put it over us, hoping to keep us somewhat warmer from the cold January air. I leaned my head against the truck of the tree and closed my eyes slowly, starting to drift off to sleep, until I heard the sound of leaves crunching followed by the sound of a heavy breathing.

Chapter 7

I froze in my spot, not daring to move a muscle, afraid of whatever is making that noise that could have noticed me and Ben.

"Ben, wake up." I whispered, trying not to make too much noise.

He shifted in my lap, opening his big blue eyes, saying, "What? I'm still tire—"

"Shh. Be quiet. There's somebody around. And I think it's H-Hunter." His eyes shot back open, and his face wore a frantic expression.

"W-we have to get out of here." His voice trembled.

"I know, but we have to be careful not to be seen," I said slowly, getting up while pushing my back against the trunk of the tree, trying to stay hidden.

Ben stood in front of me, still hiding himself too. The sound of the heavy breathing got closer to where we stood hidden. My hands started to shake and get clammy. I could hear the sound of leaves crunching under someone's feet, and they sounded close.

"I'm scared, Cassie." As soon as Ben said that, everything stopped. The heavy breathing and the sound of crunching leaves. It was silent. I stood frozen knowing they knew we were here. That was it. Hunter was going to find us, take us back to the house, and probably kill us.

I just felt bad because of how young Ben is. He hasn't even experienced life yet. His life has just started. He's still a child. An innocent one at that too and he's about to be robbed of his childhood of his life. My life had been pretty good up until yesterday.

I'm one of the lucky ones. I have good parents who care and take care of me and Ben. I have plenty of sweet friends. Sure some of them aren't as much as others but still. I have taken my life for granted. Death was never something I'd consider at the age of seventeen. I couldn't imagine being eight and innocent to the world.

The saddest thing is that I can't even do anything about it. I can't make it better like Daddy could when there was a monster under my bed or when a boy decided to break my heart into a thousand pieces; and Mom was always there to let me cry on her shoulder. They used to tell me that everything will be alright. But now that I'm faced with the reality where monsters aren't under my bed anymore, they're right in front of me waiting for me to cave in and give up.

In this moment, there's nothing I can do but wait for life to end, praying that the after life will be pretty. That there really is a heaven waiting for me to enter.

***

I hadn't noticed that Ben was looking around the trees till I heard the words "It's a deer." I could barely hear it but was so dearly grateful for being able to. I turned around the tree to see none other than a white-tailed deer, standing before us and chewing on some dead grass below its hoofs. I couldn't help when a smile spread across my lips.

"A deer," I said with joy.

"It's only a deer." I breathed out a sigh of relief.

It looked up from munching on the now dead grass. It's breath was making a small cloud of fog as it exhaled through its nose. It was a beautiful sight for I had never been this close to a deer. She looked like she was scared and at any second would just run away from us. We were her problems like Hunter was mine and Ben's.

"It's okay," I said, holding out my hand, trying to show it that I meant no harm. It still looked frightened but not as bad.

"I want to pet her," Ben asked, looking up at me.

"I don't know if she'll let you," I said back, looking down at Ben.

"I promise I won't hurt you," Ben said, holding out his hand slowly while walking to the beautiful creature in front of him. "I promise," his sweet little boy voice said comfortingly.

"I don't break my promises. Never." I just stood back, staring in awe as the little blonde-headed boy neared slowly the animal and gently laid his small hand on the deer'shead softly, petting it.

He smiled at the deer, amazed at how he was actually touching this normally frightened animal. I too was amazed at the sight. This was supposed to be a frightening moment—a moment of tears and begging for our lives—but instead we're experiencing something magical.

A boy connecting with a beautiful animal should have run ages ago. I'm never taking life for granted anymore. I'm going to live as if there's no tomorrow. Like this moment could be my last,

and I only hope Ben will do the same. I have a good feeling he will. This is a beautiful moment that I think he will cherish forever deep into his heart.

Chapter 8

Hunter Lee Stiles

I stood back watching from afar the sight of Cassandra and Ben standing before a small white-tailed deer. Ben slowly put his hand on the deer's head, petting the beautiful creature. The small deer's beauty couldn't compare to the beautiful creature named Cassandra, though.

She intrigues me.

I don't know what it is though. Maybe it's her long, curly locks of hair that cascades down her small petite body and reaches just above her perfectly shaped bum or maybe it's her forest green eyes that pull me in every time I dare to look into them.

Or could it be her soft, smooth skin that feels like silk under the touch? Or is it her... purity? Something I dream of taking.

"Stop it, Hunter! This isn't you," I scream at myself.

"But it is," I said back, the darker side of me showing its true colors.

"You don't want to hurt Cassandra, do you?"

"Why wouldn't I?" The darker me spoke back.

I do this all the time, fighting with "him"—the one that controls my actions, the one everyone sees as crazy or psychotic. It's like a never-ending battle, and yes, sometimes, my thoughts are darkened for he tells me how great it is and how much more fun life is.

"Cassandra never did anything to you," I said back, hoping to convince this so called "me."

"No, but she will just like everyone else did."

"No, she won't so just leave them alone." I reasoned.

"Yes, she will!" he yelled back.

"No, she won't, why can't you just understand that?"

"Yes, she will!" The darker "me" yelled no longer in my mind but out loud.

Cassandra and Ben's heads snapped up in my direction. There were frightened expressions as soon as they saw who it was.

"Now look what you did!" I yelled at him.

"Oh, shut the hell up!" he boomed back.

"I said, game on, Cassandra; and guess what, I never lose!" he said, running towards them.

Cassandra quickly grabbed their things, took hold of Ben's hand, and run as fast as their legs could take them.

"Stop. You're scaring them!" I yelled. "This isn't you, Hunter," I finished.

"Yes, it is me! And you're me too! Unfortunately." He said the last part out loud.

He was right. I was him and he was me. We are one but it's like two different brains with two different thoughts and actions. All he wanted to do was harm Cassandra. Like in the bathroom, I was the one who made us get the piece of glass out of her foot; but he was the one who started to dig deeper even after the glass was out. He was trying to make her cry, wanting to see the pain she was in to be written on her beautiful face. I couldn't stand to watch it

anymore so with all my will power, I made him stop his actions by running out of the small bathroom hall.

"Once I get a hold of you Cassandra, I'm going to put you through so much pain you'll be begging for me to stop!" He laughed evilly.

"I didn't mean that—" I tried to yell out only to be stopped by him.

"I said shut the hell up!"

Cassandra

I and Ben were just standing there petting the white-tailed deer when all of a sudden I heard someone yell.

"Yes, she will!" I quickly turned to where the voice was coming from only to wish I hadn't.

About thirty feet away stood the man Hunter.

"Now look what you did!" Hunter yelled suddenly.

What's his problem? I knew he was crazy but like really? Talking to himself?

"Oh shut the hell up!" A much deeper and darker voice boomed throughout the forest.

I didn't even have time to think before the same raspy voice yelled again. "I said, game on, Cassandra, and guess what, I never lose!" With that, I quickly gathered our things, threw them in the backpack, gripped Ben's small arm, and dragged him further into the woods, not daring to look back for I know he's chasing us.

"Cassandra," Ben's soft voice spoke.

"Yes?" I said, trying to keep my breathing even though it was close to impossible for my asthma was still acting up.

"We're going to die, aren't we?"

My heart broke, knowing he was right, but I couldn't let him know I thought of the same thing. I must be strong and be a good role model. I blinked the few tears back and put on my best smile as I said, "I promised, didn't I?" He nodded.

"I don't break my promises either." I reassured. I turned back to look at where I was going only to hear Hunter's voice yell again.

"Once I get of hold of you Cassandra, I'm going to put you through so much pain you'll be begging for me to stop!" An evil laugh left his lips.

"I didn't mean that—" He didn't mean that?

What is wrong with that man? I turned, completely facing ahead of me and making sure I don't trip and fall or hit a tree. I turned around to be surprised that Hunter was falling behind. He's probably a good 25-feet behind us. Just as I smile, thinking everything was going to be fine, the unthinkable happened. I heard a gun, fire but it didn't hit me.

I felt Ben's grip loosen till nothing was holding on there.

I turned to find Ben lying face down.

"Ben!" I cried.

Hunter shot Ben.

Hunter shot my brother.

Hunter shot Ben.

Chapter 9

There are times in your life when a certain someone comes into your world—either for the better or for the worse. Hunter is that someone. My life was perfectly fine two days ago. My biggest concern was how long I would possibly be grounded for forgetting to pick up my younger brother from school. The same brother who I could say I envied. I envied him because I wished to be young again—when the biggest choice I ever had to make was which piece of candy I wanted from Walmart's small checkout line or when the biggest fight I would ever get into with my friends was who got a certain Barbie. Now I'm faced with a choice. One that could change my life forever.

Laying before me was Ben, the blue-eyed eight-year-old boy who was full of life and joy and just pure happiness. But now he lay there with tears streaming from those ocean blue pools. He was holding his right thigh tightly as blood stained his blue jeans. I just stood there in shock, trying to process it all, and then it clicked. Hatred, rage, pissed. It all hit me at once, and it's all towards the man who had shot my little brother, Hunter. I run over to where he's pacing back and forth, mumbling things to himself. My fists balled up and I swung back and smacked him right in the jaw. His face turned from the impact.

"You bastard! You shot my brother!" He turned, his face back to me with a shocked and angered expression, holding his jaw tightly in his right hand.

"I-I didn't mean to!" He yelled.

"Bullshit!" I boomed back.

"You don't just accidentally shoot someone!" I yelled and pushed him backwards only for him to stumble a little then regain his balance.

He quickly grabbed me, pushing me up against a tree. His face was only inches from mine. His heavy breathing was blowing in my face.

"Don't ever hit me again," he said, slowly pushing harder on my jaw, making me wince in pain.

"And what if I do?" I dared to ask, not really caring.

"Oh, if you do, I'll kill you before you can even call for help. You'll be screaming my name to stop as I slowly drag the knife down your neck and set it right above your heart," he said slowly, dragging his index finger down my neck and stopping above my left breast.

His words frightened me. He laughs evilly at the scared expression on my face.

"Cassie." A broken voice called my name.

I turned to look at Ben. Tears were still running down his red cheeks. I tried to move under Hunter's tight grip to be able to go over by Ben but he still held me tight.

"Let me go. Please," I said, not looking away from my brother.

He leaned in and whispered in my ear, "You hit me." His breath fanned my neck.

"Why should I?" he finished.

I finally met his gaze, and a tear fell down my cheek. I had nothing to say. I knew begging wouldn't do anything so I just stood there letting the tears pour from my eyes. A few minutes later, Hunter's grip finally loosened, and he pushed me towards the direction of my brother. I almost lost my balance at the sudden movement. I quickly run over to Ben, giving him a tight hug then pulling away.

"I'm so sorry. I-I'll make it better." I reassured. I took off my jacket, ripped a strip of my blue under top, and gently wrapped it around his thigh.

He winced in pain, his eyes shutting tightly while he gripped the dead grass that laid before him.

"I'm sorry, buddy," I said, wiping away the fallen tears from my eyes.

"I-it's o-okay." He struggled to talk from the pain.

It only broke my heart more seeing him like this. He did nothing. He's an innocent to the world, he doesn't deserve this.

* * *

It's been two hours since Hunter shot Ben. It's now getting dark. I and Ben were sitting against the trunk of a tree, covered up in a blanket, while Hunter was pacing and talking to himself. I'd tried many times to tell Hunter we need to get Ben to a hospital only for him to ignore me or just shoot me a glare that could kill. I happened to find my Advil in my backpack. I quickly grabbed two small blue pills and gave them to Ben. I was not really sure if it would even help but it's better than nothing. Hunter walked back over to where we are, telling me, "We'll have to sleep here for tonight."

"Why? We can't sleep here! We don't know what's in these woods!" I fumed at him.

"Well you should have thought of that before taking off, running in here!" he shot back and was now bending so he's at my level.

"Fine." I mumbled, not wanting to anger him anymore than what he was already.

* * *

I opened my eyes when the bright January sun seeped through my tightly closed eyelids. After turning on every side, trying to keep the sun from blinding me, I finally gave up and sat up quietly. On my left was a sleeping Ben and just a few yards away, was Hunter sitting up against a tree, snoring slightly. I almost wanted to wake Ben up and make a run for home but then I remembered his leg. There's no way he would be able to walk, and I knew I couldn't carry him all the way back to the house so I decided against the idea. Then I saw something laying loosely in Hunter's right hand, the gun.

I quietly got up and moved towards him, praying to God I don't wake this man up as I got down on my hands and knees. I slowly reached for the shiny black object, gently taking it from his hand, and stood up, pointing the gun at him. He opened his eyes, looking at his hand then realizing I was standing right in front of him. Once he saw me with the gun pointed at his head, I felt like my heart had stopped. My hands were slightly sweaty. But I held my ground, aiming the gun at his head.

Chapter 10

He looked shocked that I had the gun ready to blow his brains out, and he knew why. He shot my brother and hit me and even knocked me out. He also should have thought of that before shooting my eight-year-old brother in the leg. He deserves this, but still, he is human.

All of a sudden, Hunter let out an amused laugh.

"Oh, Cassandra, what on earth are you doing?" he asked, looking up at me, smirking.

I really didn't know what I was doing. All I wanted to do was get away from him, get Ben to a hospital, and just get back to my normal life. I didn't want to shoot him but I also didn't want him to shoot one of us again so what kind of choice did I have? One, I can shoot him so me and Ben can go home and live our lives again; or two, not shoot him and possibly get shot or worse be killed by this crazy man. Either way I was going to be left with guilt so I just answered with the first thing that came to mind.

"I'm going to shoot you if you don't let me and my brother go," I said, my hands shaking slightly.

He just laughed again. What is up with him laughing? Did I not make it clear I was going to shoot him if he doesn't let us go?

That's not really something to be laughed about when you're not the one holding the gun.

"Go ahead." he said, standing up and holding out his arms, smirking.

"Go ahead, shoot me. I dare you."

I held my ground still, aiming the small pistol with my shaky hands.

"Cassie." I heard Ben's voice call my name. I turned to look at him.

"Save us," he said.

I smiled down at him, nodding.

"Yes, Cassie, go ahead save him. Shoot me, blow my brains out! Shoot me." Hunter actually sounded like he wanted me to shoot him. Was he crazy?

Oh wait, I'm pretty sure he is. I've never been a violent person. I could never kill any type of animal. The only thing I would kill are spiders, but who wouldn't kill them? I mean it's got eight legs! But he's not a spider. He's a person, a living person who has family and friends and people who care about him. He's just troubled. I can't kill a person but, I needed to save Ben. I needed to protect him.

"Go ahead. Make the same mistake I did. It's not like you'll regret it all your life," he said sarcastically.

What did he mean the same mistake?

"The thing we have in common is that if you shoot me, neither one of us knew who we were shooting. I didn't even know he was my father."

My mouth fell agape.

H-he shot his father? His head was hung low, laughing at himself.

""Why?" I asked, stepping closer to him.

He looked up at me and said, "He hurt someone I love-loved." He quickly changed his words when he realized what he had said.

"But it doesn't matter now," he finished.

"I'm sorry."

"Like I said, it doesn't matter now."

"Go ahead. If you're going to shoot me, there's no need to wait all day." I took a step back, I couldn't do this.

I can't live a life knowing I killed someone.

"I-I c-can't," I admitted as I sit down, put my head in my hands, and dropped the gun beside me.

I just couldn't kill someone. I felt him leaning down and whispering in my ear. "Stupid, stupid girl." He grabbed the gun, standing back up. I looked up at him.

"Get up." he ordered.

"Why?" I asked

"We're leaving town."

Chapter 11

"W-what? No," I protested, standing up from my sitting position on the snow-covered ground.

"No." Hunter looked back at me.

"Yes." I walked over to where Ben was sitting.

"I don't want to go with him," Ben said with worry laced in his words.

"I know. I don't either." I said, giving him a tight hug.

"Up now. We're leaving." Hunter's stern voice spoke. I looked up at him saying,

"No, you can't make us." The look of amusement played on his hard features.

"Get your ass up. Now," he ordered, pointing the small handgun at me and Ben.

I shot him the best death glare I could muster and got up slowly, helping Ben off the ground trying to support his small body. Once Ben's arm was wrapped around my shoulder, we started to follow Hunter the way we came. Hunter seemed pretty pissed off for his strides were so long I practically had to drag Ben to keep up with him.

* * *

We'd been walking for about two hours and my legs felt like jelly from not eating much plus walking for so long. Poor Ben looked in pain. I felt so bad. Hunter should let me take him to the hospital when we get back or he may be missing his genitals.

"Can you please slow down?" I asked, stopping behind Hunter. He turned around.

"We're almost there so no," he said dully, and continued walking.

"Asshole," I muttered under my breath.

Hunter stopped dead in his tracks and slowly turned around.

"What did you just call me?" he said, walking over to me.

"I think you heard me perfectly fine," I spat back.

He laughed then looked back at me.

"Oh, Cassandra, what will I do with you?"

"Let us go?" I asked, looking at him.

"I think not, sweetie." He laughed, turning around then walking forward again.

I let out a groan. Why won't he just let us go? We walked maybe ten more minutes till we're out of the woods and in the field behind my house. We walked through the short field until we reached the back porch. I carefully helped Ben up the steps, trying not to hurt his leg any more than it already was.

"Ow," he said, closing his eyes tight.

"I'm sorry buddy."

After a few more steps, we were at the back door. Hunter walked in since the door wasn't locked.

"Get your things. We're leaving in an hour," Hunter said, plopping down on the couch in the living room, putting his feet up on the coffee table.

I just shook my head while I helped Ben up stairs, taking him to his room.

"Are we really going to go with him?" Ben spoke for the first time since we got back home.

"I-I think we have to, buddy. I really wouldn't want you getting shot again."

He nodded his head looking down.

"You alright?" I asked, putting my hands on each one of his now red cheeks from being outside in the cool air.

"Yeah, I-I just miss Mom and Dad," he said, trying to hold back tears but they come pouring down his chapped cheeks anyways.

I pulled him in for a tight hug, rocking him back and forth.

"Shh, it'll be okay, don't cry." I cooed him, stroking his back to calm him down.

Mom always used to do that to me when I was upset.

"We'll get out of this mess I promise." I was hoping my words were true. That we would get away from Hunter and go back to our normal life.

Hunter

I stood outside Ben's room, listening to Cassandra telling Ben that it'll be okay. I could hear him crying as Cassie rocked him back and forth, comforting him. It didn't really bother me that he was crying till I heard a much quieter sob. I looked up to see tears streaming down Cassandra's small cheeks as she tried to hold them back.

"You did this." I spoke to "him".

"It doesn't matter," he snapped back.

"But you're hurting her. And she hasn't done anything to you."

"She will though," he spoke.

"You don't know that, you need to trust her. She could help us," I reasoned.

"She won't! She don't want to help me. Nobody does. They just hurt us, you and me, they hurt us. Don't you know that by now?"

She's different was all I said.

"How so? She'll just be afraid of us like everyone else is."

"Yes, she is afraid, of you, because you give her no reason not to be. You…you just need to show her the real you," I said truthfully.

"This is the real me and I'm never changing that because she'll never understand us. She'll never help us, and she'll never want us!"

Chapter 12

Cassandra

I held Ben in my arms for a few more minutes before getting up and packing him some clothes since he really couldn't. I took out some shirts and pants and put them in a blue suitcase then grabbed some under clothes followed by a tooth brush. I looked around his room trying to see if I missed anything. My eyes landed on his bed where his favorite stuffed animal Teddy sat. I walked over to it, picked up the small fluffy animal, and put it in the suitcase, zipping it up.

"I'm going to go pack my things. Do you want me to help you with anything else?" I asked, looking at Ben.

"No, you go pack," he said, sitting on the bed.

With that I walked over to my room, opening the door. I let out a scream as I saw Hunter sitting on my bed with his legs crossed, smirking up at me.

"Y-you scared me." I breathed out, putting my hand over my heart.

He just laughed as he stood up and walked over to me. I took a step back only to hit the half-open door behind me. He was now standing in front of me, his piercing green eyes burning through my brownish green ones. He reached behind me, pushing the door all the way shut. He leaned down and whispered in my ear, "You're still in trouble for running away and trying to shoot me." I stood still not daring to move. "And you're going to get it later." With that he backed up, pushed me to the side, and left my room, slamming the door behind him.

I stood there in shock, not moving a muscle. The only thing I was thinking was I'm going to die later.

After sitting on my bed, thinking about how I was going to get Hunter to forgive me, I decided to pack since we were leaving in about twenty minutes. I walked over to my closet, got my purple suitcase out and laid it on the bed. I then went back to my closet and got out some long-sleeved shirts and pants followed by a couple pairs of leggings and sweat shirts. After grabbing my toothbrush and hairbrush, all I had left to get was my undergarments. Once they were packed, I zipped up the suitcase, and I sat on my bed, making sure I didn't forget anything. Then I remembered something.

I went back to the closet and dug into the back, feeling around for something metal. I pulled out my crutches from last year when I broke my leg from playing volleyball. I tried telling the PE teacher that I couldn't play but she didn't believe me and made me play anyways. I grabbed my suitcase and walked over to Ben's room to find him asleep. I didn't want to wake him but I knew I had to. I plaed my suitcase down at the foot of his bed and walked over to him with the crutches in my hands.

"Hey, buddy, wake up," I said, shaking him slightly.

"Hmmm," he mumbled.

"Come on, we got to go." He opened his eyes, sitting up.

"Here, I found my old crutches, I thought you could use them." I said, holding them up.

He got out of bed, and I adjusted the crutches to the lowest sitting so he could use them without them being too tall for him.

"Hey, it actually helps," he said, walking around with them.

"Thought they might," I said picking up my suitcase and his.

We walked down the stairs. He was having a little trouble since he hadn't ever used crutches before. Hunter was on the couch, sitting with his feet up on the coffee table. He stood when he saw us.

"We're, uh... Ready," I said, looking down.

"Where did he get those crutches?" he asked.

"They were mine." He nodded, and we walked out of the house.

I took one last look as I went through the front door. I would probably never see this house again. The house in which I grew up in. I have never lived anywhere else. Parked in front of our house was a big black vehicle. I couldn't really tell what kind it is. The windows are tinted so dark that I couldn't even come close to seeing what's inside.

Hunter opened the trunk by pushing a button inside the car. I put Ben's and my bag in the trunk then helped Ben in the car, shutting the door behind him. I went over to the passenger's side, got in, and buckled my seatbelt.

"So where are we going?" I asked, looking over at Hunter who sat with his hands on the steering wheel and cigarette between his index and middle finger, blowing out a puff of smoke which made me want to gag at the smell.

"London," he simply, said blowing the smoke in my face.

Chapter 13

My mouth fell agape at his words.

"L-London?" I asked. He smirked, blowing another puff of smoke in my direction.

I looked at Ben to see a worried look written on his face. I mouthed, "we'll be okay," and he nodded. I looked back to Hunter to see he had started his car, and was turning around to drive down our long graveled driveway. It went for maybe a mile or more. That's why I thought it would be a better idea to run away from Hunter by going into the woods because by the time we would maybe get 50 yards, he would be in his car and on his way to get us.

The rest of the ride down our drive way was silent. The only sound was Hunter's heavy breathing. Occasionally, a cough would escape my lips due to the smoke-filled air that made my asthma act up, plus with the window only slightly cracked, it's really stuffy in here. We drove for a little longer before Hunter finally spoke.

"You might want to get comfortable." His raspy voice broke the awkward silence.

"Why?" I asked, looking over at him.

"It's a long drive to New York."

I let his words sink in before speaking, "B-but I thought we were going to London."

"We are but we're boarding the plane in New York." he said, throwing his cigarette out the window and turning back to me with an amused expression while my face only held shock.

"But New York is like forever away." I said, looking at him. I had been to NYC before on vacation, and it was even a long plane ride.

"Only nineteen hours," he said, smirking at me then looking back at the road

"N-nineteen hours?" I stuttered.

"Yeah, now shut up," he snapped., Bipolar much?

I sat back more comfortably in the leather seat, hoping this would be a quick trip even though nineteen hours isn't really a quick trip.

My mind started to think about my parents and what they're doing. I wonder if they miss us. I wonder how many lives my dad has saved. I remember him telling me a couple of days before he left that there were some really sick people over there and they were in need of his skillful hands. I think he said someone needed heart surgery and that there wasn't anyone there that could do such a surgery. It's pretty amazing that my father gets to work on the human heart. He always said it's a tricky thing to understand but once you do and learn that without it you are nothing, it makes you want to help that person even more. He always told me the heart is a powerful thing because it can trick you into thinking you have feelings for something or someone. "Never let the heart trick you into thinking you have feelings towards someone you actually don't," he told me once. As his way of warning me about boys, he would always say that I'm a very beautiful girl, that I deserve someone who will treat me right, and that I keep my heart safe for it's very important. He wants the man I end up with to treat me like a precious heart, like without me he is nothing.

I sank back even more into the now warm leather seat, relaxing my mind, leaving behind my father's words and putting them back into the corner of my heart. The only thing I could think of was that I'd be stuck in this car with Hunter for nineteen hours.

Chapter 14

I woke up to the sound of someone yelling. It sounded pretty pissed. I turned in my seat, opening my eyes, to see Hunter looking back at Ben and shouting something to him. I fully woke up when I realize what's going on.

"Hunter!" I yelled, now sitting fully up in my seat. He turns to me with an angered expression playing on his hard features.

"What?" he yelled back, pulling over on the side of the road.

"Why are you yelling at Ben?" I asked.

"Because your little brother didn't use the bathroom before we left the house so now he's yelling to go to the restroom!" Really. He's so mad at Ben because he had to use the restroom?

"Well, let him go to the bathroom!"

"No! J-just shut up!" He yelled, his hands hitting the steering wheel.

"Just let him use—"

"I said shut up," he said, through gritted teeth. His breathing was heavy, and his jaw was clammed shut.

After a couple of minutes of just him sitting there, staring out at the road, he finally started to pull back on the highway. I didn't dare speak, afraid he might snap again. I looked back at Ben to see he had his legs crossed and eyes shut tightly. He must really have to go.

I turned back around to look out at the road to see we we're pulling up at a gas station. Hunter parked his car at one of the pumps and turned to me. "Make it quick," he said through clenched teeth.

"Or what?" I dared to ask, pushing his buttons.

He didn't say anything and just pulled out a small gun from under his belt and smiled evilly at me.

"Come on. Let's go Ben," I said not looking away from Hunter.

I heard Ben's door open and I took that as my cue to get out as well. I slammed the door behind me and opened the front door for Ben since he couldn't because of his crutches. He hurried and went straight for the men's bathroom.

I decided I should probably go as well. I walked in, going for the stall at the end of the ladies restroom. After using the restroom, I washed my hands and face. I looked like I was warmed over shit, to be honest. My hair was in knots because I forgot to brush it today. I had dark circles under my eyes from lack of sleep, and my clothes could benefit from a good washing. I have to get me and Ben out of this mess. There's no way I'm getting back in that car with Hunter.

I walked out of the ladies restroom to see Ben sitting on a bench beside the men's bathroom. He stood up when he saw me, and asked, "We're not getting back in the car with Hunter, are we?" I looked him straight in the eyes and said, "Hell no." He smiled one of the biggest smiles I've ever seen on him. I grabbed his crutches, handing them to him, and walked over to the cash register.

"Hi, um, can I use your phone real quick?" I asked, motioning to the cellphone that sat on the counter.

"Uh, sure, make it quick though," the lady said.

I nodded. She handed me her phone, and I took it, dialing mom's number. It rang a few times.

"Come on, pick up," I spoke through the phone, looking outside to see Hunter getting gas.

"Hello." I heard my mother's sweet voice speak through the phone.

"Mom! Oh my gosh, you have to help us," I gushed through the speaker.

"What is it, sweetie?"

"There's this man, he-he took us a-and his name is Hunter," I said as fast as I could, afraid he might come in here any minute.

"What!" My mother yelled, frantic.

"And h-he's taking us to London—" I was cut off by the phone being snatched from my hands. I looked up to see a pissed off Hunter.

Chapter 15

Hunter grabbed my upper arm and gave the women her phone back before pulling me out of the small gas station. Ben was following close behind. Hunter flung the passenger-side door open and pushed me in. I was about to tell Ben not to get in the car so we could just make a run for it, but by the time I turned around Hunter was already in the driver's seat. He gripped the steering wheel so tight that his knuckles and hands were starting to turn white.

"What the hell was that?" he yelled, turning to look at me.

I quickly turned away from him and just looked out of the window. He started to pull out of the gas station's parking lot.

"Who were you talking to?" he asked through gritted teeth.

I didn't say anything.

"I asked you a question!" He snapped, gripping my jaw and turning my face to look at him.

I could feel the tears coming but I held them back by closing my eyes tightly.

"Who. Were. You. Talking. To." He repeated, pausing between each word.

"M-my mom," I croaked out.

He now held my jaw even tighter with his large hand.

"Don't ever do that again," he told me and slapped my face.

The impact of the hit caused my face to fly towards the passenger's window. I let the tears pour freely, not caring who saw me. I stayed quiet, not daring to say anything, afraid of pissing him off even more.

I started thinking about life. What's going to happen to me and Ben? Was Hunter going to kill us? Would we ever get to see our family again? Will life ever be the same? So many questions were filling my mind that I didn't even notice that the car stopped, and smoke was coming out from under the hood.

"Shit!" Hunter cursed, his hands hitting the steering wheel.

Stupid car,"" Hunter said under his breath, getting out of the car and opening the hood.

"We're getting out of here," I said, turning to Ben. He smiled and nodded his head.

"Do you think you could run with the crutches?"

He thought for a minute. "Yeah, I think I can," he said, grabbing his crutches.

I looked back to the hood, making sure Hunter was busy before we would get out.

"I have an idea," I said, reaching over to the driver's side to pop the trunk. "Okay, we're going to go out through the trunk so he doesn't see us." Ben nodded and started to slowly crawl over the back seat.

It was a little difficult since his leg was still sore. After a few minutes we were both out of the car and running towards the highway which was just a few yards away. Cars were passing by so fast it was almost impossible to catch one's attention. We waved our hands in all different directions, hoping for one to see us and stop.

"Help!" we both yelled.

Some people would just look at us like we were crazy and others would just laugh.

"Help us please!" Ben cried.

"It's okay, Ben, we'll get someone's attention," I said, not looking away from the road. "I promise, buddy. You know I don't break my promises, right?" I asked, still waving my hands in the air, but there was no reply.

I turned around, and I could already feel the tears building up from the sight in front of me. Hunter had a gun pointed to Ben's head.

Chapter 16

It felt as if my heart had fallen out as the scene in front of me was playing. Hunter had a gun pointed to Ben's head. My brother's head. My little brothers head! Why him? He did nothing wrong. He only followed me. There is no need for this, for Hunter to hold a pistol to Ben's head.

I stood there frozen, with tears falling, as Hunter held Ben tightly behind the car. I'm guessing he did that so nobody could see what he was doing. If only someone could.

"H-Hunter, p-please l-let B-Ben g-go," I croaked out, slowly walking towards the crazy man that was holding my brother.

A raspy laugh left Hunter's cruel lips. "You really think I'm just going to let him go after that little stunt you just pulled?" he asked, smirking at me.

"Please." I cried.

"He didn't do anything. He's only a child, Hunter!" I yelled, anger boiling through my veins.

"Well since you put it that way," he said, his words dripping with sarcasm.

Silence filled the air. Only the sound of passing cars behind me could be heard.

"Okay, I'll make you a deal," he said. I walked even closer to him 'til I was only three feet away from him.

"And that is?" I asked, wiping the tears that had fallen.

"I'll let Ben go like for good," he told me, making a smile creep its way on my lips.

"Really?" I asked, excited to know that Ben would get to be let free. At least one of us can get away from this horrible person.

"Yes really, but under one condition," he said, smirking once again.

"And what might that be?"

"You must stay with me and do whatever I say." His words stung. I would have to follow and do as Hunter says for an unlimited amount of time, but if it would mean Ben would be free then so be it.

"Fine. Now let my brother go," I said, reaching for Ben's arm that was outstretched towards me.

"Patience, Cassandra," he said, smiling evilly at me.

Hunter pulled out his phone from his back pocket while still holding onto Ben tightly. He tapped the touch screen a few times before putting it to his ear.

"We're ready for you. Yes now. Okay, see you in a few," he said into the speaker of the phone before ending the call.

"Who was that?" I asked, looking at him suspiciously.

"That's for me to know," he said, opening the back seat door.

"And for you to never find out," he finished and closed the door.

"But—"

"No buts," he simply said before grabbing my arm and putting me in the backseat as well.

We waited for probably fifteen minutes before a big black SUV pulled up beside us. Two men got out of the vehicle. They look about the same age as Hunter. I'm guessing about twenty or so. One of the men had blonde hair and brown roots, you could tell he dyed it. The other man had brown hair and bluish green eyes. They both were wearing all black clothing similar to Hunter's outfit.

"Where is the boy?" The brown-headed man asked.

"In the backseat," Hunter replied, opening the door near Ben.

Both men looked carefully at Ben then look in my direction smiling.

"What happen to his leg?" The blonde asked, not looking away from Ben's wrapped up leg.

"I shot him," Hunter said, scratching the back of his neck

"Why?" the other man now asked.

"That doesn't matter—"

"For no reason," I said, now being the one smirking.

Hunter just gave me his best death glare. I looked away from his deadly stare and turned my attention back to the men.

"Okay," they said, looking away from Ben's bandaged leg.

"We'll take him from here," The brown-headed guy said, making me turn my full attention to him.

"W-what?" I asked, starting to get worried.

"Shut up, Cassie," Hunter hissed.

"I can speak if I want, and don't call me Cassie!" I yelled, staring right at Hunter.

"Did you already forget our little deal, Cassie?" *It's Cassandra*, I think to myself, *bastard*.

"You know the deal about how you have to do whatever I say?" he said, letting that all too familiar smirk play on his hard features.

I keep quiet after that. He was right, I did agree to that stupid deal not even an hour ago.

"That's what I thought," he told me, turning back around to face the men.

"Come on, kid," the blonde said, grabbing on to Ben's arm and pulling him out of the car.

"Where are you taking him? I thought you said you were letting him free," I asked, frightened at what he might reply with.

"One, that doesn't matter, and two, I lied," he said, laughing evilly once again.

"W-what? No, you can't!" It was too late, though, Ben was already dragged out of the car.

"Cassie!" Ben cried.

"Ben!" I yelled as the door was shut and locked.

I tried to open it to save Ben, but it was too late. He was pushed into the SUV. I screamed his name, banging on the window for them to bring him back, but it was no use. He was gone. Ben was gone.

Chapter 17

"You monster! I hate you!" I yelled as Hunter shut his door.

"You liar! You're a liar!" I cried, he just looked at me through the mirror above the dash.

"Shut the hell up, Cassie, before I send you off with some man."

"Well he probably would be a heck of a lot better a man than you!" I spat back.

"No, no he wouldn't, because what all men like him would want to do is just hurt you in ways you would never forget." His words caught me off guard, knowing exactly what he meant.

"Well isn't that what all of you want to do? Hurt me?" I yelled, no longer having any room for tears. Only range could be seen on my soft features.

"No... No, Cassandra, I don't."

What scared me the most was how serious he was while he said those few simple words that I should be grateful for hearing, but really they only scare me even more.

There's not one man on this earth who doesn't think about sex and banging a girl so why was he saying that? Because he's a liar. He even admitted it, he's lying.

"You probably think I'm lying, don't you?" he said it like he was reading my thoughts.

"Yes," I honestly said.

"Well I'm not, Cassandra. I'm not, I promise." He almost sounded believable, but I wasn't going to believe that sorry bastard.

"I know you don't believe me, I understand. I probably wouldn't either if I was in your place but you just have to believe in that one thing, okay?" He asked me, still looking at me through the mirror.

"No," I simply said. "I can't. You gave me no reason so why should I?"

"Because it's the truth, Cassandra. If you don't believe me then believe this. When I was fourteen I saw my mother go through something I hope no women will ever have to endure. I'm not going to do what that man did to my mother to you. Okay?" He looked like he was on the verge of tears, but I know him enough to know he wouldn't let one tear fall from those cruel cold eyes of his.

I didn't say anything and just looked back out the window, letting the tears fall for so many reasons. Ben, will I ever see him again? Will I ever see my family again? Will Hunter ever let me go? I didn't know the answer to any of those questions I had for myself, and that is one of the thing that scared me the most about life. Not knowing what's going to happen.

Life is like a horror movie. You're sitting on the edge of your seat, seeking to know what's going to happen next. You're a little afraid but also excited to know what's going to happen, but it really doesn't matter because every great horror film has an end as well as every life has its end. But what's important is making that end worth living for, same as the horror film. Its end needs to be just as good its beginning.

* * *

I woke up to the sound of someone calling my name. I slowly opened my eyes to be met with Hunter hovering above me. I jumped back at the sight.

"I'm not going to hurt you," he said, trying to sound soothing.

"Yeah, right," I said under my breath.

"Come on, we're here."

I looked up at him. "Where?"

"At the hotel where we'll be staying for the night," he told me as he got off of me and opened the car door, letting me out.

I looked up at the big sign that was lit up by lights, the sign reading "Super 8."

"Oh real fancy. You've outdone yourself, Hunter," I said sarcastically.

"Really funny. Now come on and be quiet, it's late."

I followed him into the lobby of the no-star motel only to see a young man asleep behind a desk with drool dripping from his parted mouth.

I cringe at the sight. Hunter then walked us over to the elevators. Wow, they can actually afford elevators! I'm shocked because obviously they can't afford maids for there is about an inch of dirt covering the floor. Hunter pushed the number 3 button, and before long we're out of the dirt-infested elevator and Hunter was sticking the key in the lock. I had no idea when he got the key. He probably stole it.

After the door was unlocked and opened, we walk in only to find that the room was even dirtier than the rest of the hotel areas that we had seen so far. I would hate to see what the bathroom looks like. After looking at the nasty, hairy floor, my eyes landed on the one single-sized bed placed in the middle of the room. Only one thing was going through my mind. Hell no.

Chapter 18

I stood in the middle of the room, staring at the bed then looking around hoping to find some kind of small couch or even a chair, anything. Anything would be better than sharing a bed with that cruel man who sent my little brother off to God knows where.

"Well don't just stand there," Hunter said, snapping me out of my thoughts.

"Uh... Yeah." I breathed out, walking over to the bed and sitting down as far away from the curly one as I could.

"Don't be so distant," He commented, scooting closer till his thigh was touching mine.

I stood up as soon as I felt the contact.

"I-I'm going to take a shower," I said, and ran off to the bathroom, locking the door behind me.

The bathroom wasn't terribly dirty but you could still see hair all over the floor and counter. I quickly stripped and turned the shower, getting in the steaming hot water which relaxes my muscles. When I had washed my hair with some shampoo, I grabbed the bar of soap and started cleaning myself. After rinsing off, I got out and grabbed a towel from under the sink and began to dry my body. I quickly realize that I hadn't brought any clothes in the bathroom with me. I wasn't about to put on my old ones. I could go out there in my towel and run to get them, hoping Hunter doesn't see, or I could ask him to bring me some.

I was too afraid to run out there for he would probably try and pull down the fabric which covered my body so I decided that I would just ask him to bring me some clothes. I slowly unlocked the door and cracked it open, just enough so I could see he that he was sprawling on the bed, looking up at the ceiling.

"H-Hunter..." I trailed off in a quiet voice. He rose from the bed, looking at me through the crack in the door.

"Yes, Cassie," he said, smirking. God I hate when he calls me that.

"Uh, c-could you bring me some clothes?" I stuttered like an idiot.

He got off the bed. "Sure thing, love." I watch as he walked over to my suitcase that I had packed earlier.

He unzipped it, digging through, and after about three minutes of him just looking through my clothes, he walked over to the door.

"Here,"" he said, looking me straight in the eyes until his green pools diverted their attention downward.

I snatched my clothes from him and tried shutting the door only for it to be caught. I looked up to see Hunter's foot in the way of the door.

"Move please," I whispered, not looking away from his black shoe.

"Don't be too long, baby." His words angered me. I wasn't his "baby" or "love."

He moved his foot out of the way. I quickly shut the door, locking it then dropping the towel. I picked up the bra and panties he had picked out for me. They were my black lacy ones with open sides. The bra was solid jet black except that the thin straps had little jewels. I quickly put them on, not being able to do anything about them. I should have known that he would pick them. I slipped the shorts on. I see he had found it buried deep down in my suitcase.

I put the sweat shirt on then walked back out to see that the overhead light was off, the only light being the lamp on the nightstand. Hunter had his back on me. I walked over to the bed slowly, getting in and moving as far away from him as I could get. As much as I hate that I had to sleep with him, I knew there was nowhere else I could go. I lay on my back, staring at the ceiling, not really thinking about anything. I felt the bed move and saw Hunter was up. He walked over to his jacket, pulling out a pack of cigarettes. He laid them down on the nightstand beside me and lifted his shirt over his head. I couldn't help but look. He has tattoos running up his neck. I spotted the "I'm sorry" one on his collarbone.

"Like what you see?" Hunter asked, looking down at me, smirking again.

"Uh..." I didn't know what to say so I just looked away and kept my eyes on the ceiling.

A few seconds later I felt the bed dip down. I looked at Hunter from the corner of my eye to see he was lighting a cigarette.

"You want one or something?" he asked, looking over at me.

"N-no. No," I said quickly.

"Goody goody." He laughed under his breath.

"Yes, yes I am," I proudly admitted. I wasn't ashamed of being a goody goody.

It was silent for probably ten minutes before I decided to ask a brave question for me.

"Hunter."

"Yes?" he replied, turning his body so he was facing me.

"Um, w-what does your tattoo mean?" I asked shyly, hoping not to anger him.

"Which one? I have a few." He laughed.

"The one that says I'm sorry." His face went hard and he stopped moving.

"It's kind of my way of saying sorry for things I've done," he told me, looking away.

"Is there one thing in particular?" I bravely pushed further.

"Sort of," He said simply.

"I got it after I killed my father."

"Why did you k-kill your father?" I stuttered, now regretting sharing a bed with him.

"Reasons. Now go to sleep," he bluntly snapped.

I did what I was told and turn on my side with my back facing him.

Chapter 19

I woke from a sharp pain running through my wrist. I tried moving them only to realize that I was getting nowhere. I looked up only to see that my wrists were handcuffed to the headboard. I tried to pull my hands towards me, hoping to get out of them but it only made the pain worse. I couldn't believe Hunter cuffed me to the bed. I turned around enough to see over my shoulder only to find that no one was there.

So the idiot left me, cuffed me to the bed while he went to only God knows where. I lay there since there's nothing else I could really do. My thoughts start to take my mind to places. Where is my little brother? Is he alright? Is he even alive? Are those men going to kill him? I didn't know and I so wish I did. I miss my brother. I never meant for this to happen. Hunter said he would let him go, that he would be free. I thought at least one of us would be let go, but no, Hunter had to lie. He lied about letting my brother go free, and I will never be able to forgive him for doing such a thing. I lay there, letting the tears pour. I messed up. I'm the reason that Ben isn't here right now with me. It's all my fault.

All of a sudden the hotel door flew open to a fuming Hunter. He looked really pissed. His breathing was uneven and heavy and his hair was a mess. It looked like he was pulling at it. He looked at me, anger could be seen in his eyes. I sank back into the bed, hoping he wouldn't come over, but unfortunately he did. He stormed over to me.

"Get up!" he yelled at me.

"I-I c-can't," I say, motioning to the hand cuffs.

He began digging in his pocket, trying to find something. After a few seconds, he pulled out a small key and threw it at me. It landed on my lap. Is he stupid or something? I couldn't un-cuff myself.

"H-Hunter," I whisper. He turned and looked at me, obviously still pissed.

I looked down at the key then back at my cuffed hands, hoping he would get the hint. His breathing got even heavier before he violently grabbed the chains and stuck the key in the lock. Once my hands were let free, he grabbed me by the arms, pulled me out of the bed, and threw me on the ground. All I could think was what did I do. He started to pace in the hotel room, pulling his curls and mumbling things to himself. I just sat there, not wanting to do anything to make him even more mad.

"You're so stupid!" he yelled all of a sudden, looking at me. Before I could respond he continued. "Calling your mom, and now the cops are after me! My face and yours are plastered all over the damn news!" he finished and looked back at me. He got down to my level on the dirty floor and put both his hands on my cheeks.

"You're a very brave girl to mess with me but never forget that I never lose."

The cops will find me and Ben, and he will go to jail for a very long time. It'' just when will the cops find me. A few?

Minutes pass before Hunter finally spoke. "Get up we're leaving," He spat, grabbing his cigarettes on the nightstand.

I did as I was told. I got up from the floor, putting my shoes and coat on. He grabbed everything else that is ours before leaving the hotel room and walking to the car. I got into the passenger's side, shutting the door and buckling up. Hunter did the same except he didn't wear his seatbelt. It bugged me that he didn't. Even though I hate him with a great passion, I still wanted the bastard to put his seatbelt on.

"Y-you might want to p-put that on—"

"Shut up." He snapped, not giving my comment a second thought.

We drove for probably two hours before we pulled up to an alley where music was blaring from a door just a few feet away. The sign read "Inked Queen." I stared at the sign, wondering why Hunter would bring me here.

"What are we doing here?" I asked, still staring at the building.

"Getting a new look." he said, smirking at me.

Chapter 20

I stared at him in utter shock. He can't seriously mean we're getting a new look! Can he?

"Well don't just sit there and stare at me. I mean I know I'm gorgeous and all but get your shit together. Can't have you gawking at me all day." He laughed.

"Stuck on our self much, are we?" I asked as I got out of the car, sending him his famous smirk he always seems to use on me.

"Well when you're this hot it's kind of hard not to be," he shot back, getting out of the car and walking over to the alley where the loud so called music was coming from.

I followed closely behind as I saw some tattooed and pierced people who didn't look too friendly or at least didn't let on to be. I tried smiling at a young girl but she just gave me the finger.

Real classy, I think. Hunter opened the door, well not for me because he just waltzed right on in, leaving the door to slap me in the face.

"What a gentleman," I said sarcastically as I quickly opened the door to catch up with Hunter.

You wouldn't want to lose someone in this type of place. The first thing I saw as I enter the building was the strobe lights. They're the one kind of light I could live without. They're so confusing and they always give me one hell of a headache. Once by Hunter's side, I started to take in my surroundings a little more instead of focusing on the blinding lights. There's a dance floor where girls in very little clothes are so called dancing, but really they just looked like they're rubbing their bodies up against one other. I looked away, disgusted by the scene, and let my pure eyes wander somewhere else. To my left was a bar where guys and girls were taking shots and drinking who knows what.

Hunter grabbed my hand as we came up on the dance floor. For a second I thought he was going to make me start rubbing himself all over me. Instead, he just held my hand tightly and pulled me through the grinding crowd. Once we were finally away from the sweaty bodies, he pulled me into a curtained room where a girl, probably around the age of twenty, sat, cleaning some kind of tattooing tools. Oh, wonderful." I think he's going to make me get a tattoo. The girl looked up from cleaning her tools after she saw us came in.

"Hunter!" Her high-pitched voice could break glass, no doubt about that.

I had only heard her say one word and I already hate the girl, bad I know, but God that voice.

Her blue hair was put into some crazy rat's-nest-slash-bun, and I'm pretty sure she couldn't get any more piercings for there's not one bare spot left on her ears or lip. Her clothing looked like ripped netting, well actually I think it is.

Hunter walked over to the blue-haired chick.

"Storm!" So her name is Storm? Who names their child Storm? Well I guess it's pretty neat considering not many people would have such a name.

"Where have you been? I've missed your ugly ass around here," she jokingly said, hitting his arm.

"You know, here and there," he told her, not making eye contact.

"I see. Who's this chick?" Storm directed her attention to me.

"Oh, um. This is Cassandra."

I walked over to the blue-haired one and extended my hand for her to shake, but she only laughed in my face.

"Sweetie, nobody shakes hands anymore." I just laughed along with them.

"So what can I do for you to day?" Storm asked, looking back at Hunter.

"We need a new look, especially her," Hunter explained, looking over at me. Storm smiled at me and said, "I can do that." And with that she took my hand and led me over to a chair and let me sit down. She told me to lean my head back so she could wash my hair. Once it was washed and shampooed, she started to put color dye in my hair.

"What color are you using?" I asked, slightly afraid.

"You like pink and purple right?" she asked, looking down at me from where she was putting the dye on.

"I… Uh..." I was too shocked to say anything.

Hunter was beside me in a chair. Just like he, he was getting something done to his hair. All I could think about was that I was going to look like one of those freaks that my dad always says to stay away from.

About an hour later, my hair was being blow dried. "Okay hair is done!" Her high-pitched voice sang.

"Okay, so I'm done?"

"Oh no, sweetie, we still have makeup!" Great. Makeup. Something I don't really wear nor like wearing.

After a purple eye shadow, a mountain of eyeliner, and a mascara she was finally done with my eyes. She applied a light pink lipstick and then some pink blush. "Done!" She cheered, clapping her hands.

"Now time for piercings and tattoos!"

"W-what?" The only piercings I have are in my ears, and I never even thought about getting a tattoo. I always thought they look a little trashy on girls.

"You would look so hot with a nose ring!" She happily screamed.

"O-okay."

Not even five minutes later, the sting was gone and I was left with a hoop pierced into my nose.

"Shouldn't it be a stud?"

"Oh no, hoops will work fine." She smiled.

"Now tattoos, what will it be?"

I really didn't know what I wanted or if I even want one. "I really don't know." I told her truthfully.

"Well it can be meaningful or it could just be something you like, maybe a butterfly, or something cute like that." she suggested.

I thought for a minute. Then it came to me I know what I want. "I think I know what I want." I said.

"Yay! How exciting!" She got her tools to do the tattoo.

I told her what I want and where I want the ink to go for the rest of my life. Once it was done, I stared down at my wrapped up pinky finger.

"Wow."" I heard a raspy voice say above me. I look up to see Hunter with the ends of his hair lightly colored blue, but that's all that I can see that is different about him.

"Blue?" I asked.

"Yeah, so you hair is like purplish pink." He was right about that, even though I still haven't dared to look in the mirror.

"So I see you got a tattoo. What'd you get?" he asked.

"I got Ben's name put on my pinky finger."

"And why'd you do that?" He sounded kind of mad.

"Well I and Ben would always pinky promise, and well I promised him that everything would be alright and I still want to keep that promise even though I have no idea where he is," I confessed, letting a tear run down my cheek.

"Get up, we're leaving." His voice now sounded stern and mean again.

"Now where are we going?" I asked.

"London. I already told you." With that he got up and paid Storm for the tattoo and hair dye.

Hunter practically dragged me out of the building, and slammed the car door shut, and sped off down the road.

Chapter 21

Hunter had been driving for probably three hours and had barely even spoke a word to me.

I was beginning to think he hates me now because I got Ben's name put on my pinky finger. I don't know why, though, it's my body. I can do what I wish with it. I don't need someone telling me that I can't do this or that. With my body, it's my choices. I mean did he think I was going to put "Hunter" on my pinky finger? No, heck no. Why would I put that pricks name on my body? All he has done is hurt me and my family and one day he will pay for what he has done.

"Are you hungry?" His voice broke my thoughts.

"Yes, I'm starving because you being the horrible man you are has barely even fed me," I think to myself. "Yeah a little bit," I replied, pushing the old thought to the back of my mind.

"What would you like?" Wow he's actually asking what I want for once.

"Food would be good."

"Well, no shit, Cassandra." he said, shaking his head.

"What about IHOP? I saw a sign for it a few miles back." he asked.

"Sure that's fine." I've never even eaten at IHOP, weird I know.

We drove for about ten more minutes before we pulled up to the small restaurant. We both got out and went in. An older lady let sat us at a small table in the back, Hunter's request. She handed us our menus and left to give us a few minutes to decide what we would like to eat.

"What do you normally get here?" Hunter broke the silence.

"I've never been here before." I admitted.

"What? You've never been here before?"

"Yep, never been," I answered.

"Well then, you will have to get the chocolate chip pancakes because they are amazing."

"Okay." And with that we sat silently till our waitress came back.

Hunter then ordered four chocolate chip pancakes and two waters. The waitress left to put the order in.

"So..." I started, breaking the silence.

"So what?" Hunter asked.

"So how old are you?"

"I'm twenty, and you?"

"Sixteen, I'll be seventeen on May seventh." I couldn't wait to be able to drive on my own.

Nice," He simply replied.

I really needed to find out more about Hunter considering I literally know nothing about him.

"Do you have any younger brothers or sisters?" I asked, looking at Hunter in the eyes.

He shifted a little in his seat and broke eye contact with me.

"Younger sister," he told me while playing with the salt shaker.

"What's her name?" I pushed further.

He put the salt shaker down and looked me in the eyes as he said, "Her name was Lily." I think I saw a tear in Hunter's eye but if there was one he must've wiped it away.

"I'm so sorry. I'm sure she's in a better place now," I said, now feeling guilty for bringing it up.

"Let's hope. It was all my fault..." He trailed off, looking away from me.

So he killed his own sister? God, this man has issues.

"There wasn't enough time. I couldn't get them out."

I was about to ask why there wasn't enough time, but before I could our waitress came with our food.

She placed the two plates of pancakes and asked us if we need anything else. Hunter replied, "No, we're fine." We eat our chocolate chip pancakes in silence.

I wanted so badly to ask why there wasn't enough time, but I knew I shouldn't so I just kept quiet. Once done eating, Hunter paid and we left. The clock in the car reads 11:56pm. It was late and we were both tired. Hunter pulled the car off to the side of the road and put it in park.

Chapter 22

"Bedtime," he said, smiling over at me. "Great," I thought.

"Sorry about having to sleep in the car. Can't afford a hotel every night," he told me, looking out at the stars through the window.

The view was beautiful for we were out in the middle of almost nowhere. I could really see the stars tonight.

"It's okay. If you didn't, I don't think we would get to see this view." I breathed out, smiling out of the window.

"True," he simply said, reaching up above our heads and pushing a button on the ceiling making the sunroof open to the galaxy above.

He let his seat leaned back, and I did the same, relaxing for the first time since he showed up at my house. It was silent for a good ten minutes before I spoke. "Hunter..." It was quiet for a second before he said anything back.

"What?"

"Why do you sometimes act... different?" I wondered, looking over at him.

"What do you mean?" I was surprised that he wasn't' angry yet with me for asking.

"Like sometimes you're sweet and kind but then other times you act like you're... psycho." I said the last word in almost a whisper.

"I-I... It's him," He tried to explain, looking away from my gaze.

"Him?" I pushed further.

"The other me..." He trailed off.

"H-he c-controls me sometimes a-and I can't do anything about it."

"He takes over." His words frightened me but I let him continue.

"It's like being two different people," he said, keeping his eyes on the stars above.

"But I don't want to talk about it anymore." He looks over to my direction.

"That's fine," I replied. It was silent for a while before I spoke again. "Will you tell me about yourself? I mean, since I'm going to be staying with you."

"I guess." He didn't really sound too sure about what he's agreeing to, but he didn't say anything about it.

"What would you like to know?" he asked, not making eye contact.

I thought for a minute. This was important. He seemed to be in a good mood. Maybe he will tell me about what happened to his sister.

"Uh... What happened to your sister? You never finished what you were going to say—"

"Something else I don't want to talk about, the past."

Well so much for that I think. "Something simple."

I thought for a second.

"What's your favorite color?" I asked, a small chuckle leaving my parted lips.

"Why are you laughing?" he asked, sitting up somewhat.

"It's just, I go from one extreme to the next," I admitted, looking into his forest green eyes.

"Well, it's black," he said, looking away from me and back out at the sunroof.

And here came the "other" Hunter.

"That's not much of a color," I whispered.

"It explains the world, my life, my soul, and my mind."

"Well my favorite color is aqua blue," I said, quickly changing the subject.

"Well that's uh... nice color," he stammered suddenly.

"Hunter," I said his name, my voice turning serious.

"Yeah?"

"W-what... Was your childhood bad?" I asked, afraid of the way he might react.

It got deadly silent after that. The only noise that could be heard was his heavy breathing. I knew in a way it was none of my business, but hell, I am going to be staying with him, I think I at least should get to know some things about this guy.

"Yes, it was bad," He admitted in almost a whisper, playing with the hem of his sweater.

"I'm sorry." I didn't mean to upset him. I just wanted to know something about this man.

"It's fine, you can't change the past. It is what it is," he replied.

It was silent again. I wondered what happened in his past. Well more than what I already knew. He told me he killed his father because he was hurting his mother and that his sister died for unknown reasons. But there had to be more since it is such a touchy subject for him. So much could have gone on, I just wanted to know. I wanted to help him.

Even though he had hurt me deep down, I knew he just needed help. I'd always been the friend to ask lots of questions and try to help my friends out on their problems by talking about them. I never was the type to tell their secrets unless it meant they were hurting themselves in some way. Then of course I would have to tell on them so their parents could get them help. I can't stand to see people going through pain.

If Hunter would just let out some of his past and talk about it instead of keeping it all in, he might change.

"Tell me about yourself. I told you some about me, now it's your turn." His voice broke my thoughts of him.

"Uh... I'm kind of a boring person," I told him, letting out a nervous chuckle. Why am I nervous?

"Come on, the famous Cassandra Lowe has to have something interesting about her."

I don't even want to know how he found out my last name. "Well I like cats..."

"so you like—"

"Hunter! Get your head out of the gutter!"

Not even two seconds later, we were both in a fit of laughter. His laugh was something else. His eyes would almost close, and he would start hitting his hand on the steering wheel while the high-pitched laugh would flow out of his parted lips. He looked... different. Happy for once.

"So is it true, you like cats?" he asked, making me smile over at him.

"Yeah, cats." I chuckled.

"Okay what else do you like other than cats?"

"Family," I simply said, looking away from him and out the window.

I could feel the tears ready to fall. I just wanted my family back. I just wanted to know that Ben is okay. I just wanted someone to tell me that it will all okay, but I have a feeling that's not going to happen.

"I'm sorry," The man beside me whispered something I thought would never escape his lips.

How could he be sorry when he did it, when he could make it all better by letting me go? How? Because he isn't.

Chapter 23

My eyes opened only to be met with plain white walls standing before me. I looked around in all directions, trying to find a door or some way out. Nothing. There was no way out. I stood to my feet, wondering where I could be. Am I in a basement? Maybe? No, can't be. There would have to be a door or some way of getting out of here. Maybe I'm in some type of prison holding room. I know I couldn't be in jail for I haven't done anything wrong. What if the police found me and Hunter then I would be let free. I could go back to my normal life, but why would they have me in here? Am I dead? I thought to myself, is this heaven? Did I really die?

Suddenly, part of the wall opened up. Walking in was a man dressed in dark clothing. He wore a black long-sleeved shirt, dark jeans, and solid black boots. The only color that I could make out other than black on the young man near my age was a red liquid dripping from his hands. He started to walk towards me. I was tempted to run away, scared of what he might possibly do. But as he neared me, he walked right past me, striding to a plain wall not far from where I was currently standing. The only sound that could be heard was his heavy footsteps and the odd sound of the scarlet liquid dripping from his large hands. The red substance left a trail behind him, deep red dots spotting the pearly white floor where we both stand on.

Once he stood before the plain wall, he looked back at me with a devilish grin playing on his lips. He looked back to the wall and started to glide his hands across it like he was painting. It didn't take long before words were formed, dripping in deep red. It's when I read the wording I, then I knew that the red liquid was blood. The wall read in bold letters, "Ben is dead."

My heart stopped and my hands began to sweat, my breathing turned rigid.

"No, this can't be true," I said to myself.

"No, it can't be." I cried, taking sharp breaths. The dark figure stareds to walk towards me and that's when I started screaming at him.

"No! He's not dead!" I screamed.

"Cassandra." The raspy voice spoke.

"No! Get away from me!" I yelled, backing away from him.

"Cassie." He sang my nickname and an evil grin played on his features.

"No!" I cried.

"Cassie, wake up!" he said, standing only five feet away.

"What?"

"Wake up, Cassie. It's only a dream." The white walls started to fade along with the dripping words and everything turned dark.

***

"Wake up, Cassandra," I opened my eyes, breathing heavily.

I quickly sat up, grabbing onto the door handle.

"Cassandra? We're boarding the plane now," I heard a voice say.

I slowly turned my head to my left only to see the man that was dressed in all black in my horrible dream. I jumped back slightly, grabbing on to the place above my left breast where my heart is.

"Are you alright?" Hunter asked, concern written on his face.

"Uh, y-yeah. L-lets g-go," I stammered, opening the car door.

He did the same with his as I walked around to the trunk of the car. He then popped the lid, raising it slowly.

"Here," he said, handing me my suitcase. I take it from him, sitting it on the ground and pulling up the handle, so it would be easier to move. I was still shaken up about the whole Ben-is-dead dream.

It makes me wonder whether he really is dead. I quickly pushed the thought to the back of my mind when I felt the tears coming. He can't be dead. That's my little brother, he is supposed to live longer than me. I couldn't imagine dying at a young age of eight. He's never done anything wrong. Yes, he has not made his bed when he was supposed to and sure he has eaten the last cookie when it was really dad', but when you really think about it, he's an innocent to the world and I couldn't imagine him dying.

After my concerned thought about my younger brother, I finally looked up to see where I was. I was expecting us to arrive at an airport, instead a large open field sat in front of me. The only thing that told me we're in the right place and Hunter didn't just stop here to kill me is that twenty feet away lays what seems to be a landing or takeoff strip. At one end of the paved road, a small engine plane was parked right in the middle.

"Well don't just stand there, come on." Hunter beckoned me as he stalked off towards the plane. My hand clutched the handle of my suitcase, and my feet followed him closely from behind. I would've made a run for it but I was almost positive I would have failed due to the fact there was literally nothing except field and more field. Hunter could easily get in his SUV and chase after me.

"Hunter! There you are. I've been waiting here for hours. What the hell took so long?" A man with a darker skin and built body asked.

"Sorry, Mikey, I had a bit of trouble getting her here." Hunter pointed towards my direction, and my eyes rolled as we continued closer towards the plane.

"Well let's not waste any more time." With that said, we got aboard the small plane and buckled in. There are only four seats so all the luggage goes inside a small compartment at the back of the plane.

Chapter 24

I decided to speak once we're up in the air. "Hunter," I whispered, slightly turning to face him.

He slowly turned his head to look me in the eyes and said, "Yes, Cassandra?" I took a deep breath, preparing for the worst of what he could reply with.

"Is Ben still... alive?" I asked, giving him my best puppy dog eyes, hoping to make him feel bad and tell me where on earth my little brother is.

"I don't know."

What killed me the most about those three words was how serious he sounded when he uttered them. He truly didn't know.

"H-how could you not know? Did you even know the men that you sent him off with?" I asked, raising my voice slightly.

He looked like he was taken aback by my little outburst. He gave me a stern look.

"Yes, I know them and I also know what they're capable of so to answer your question more clearly, I have no idea if the little shit is alive!" he yell-whispered.

I could already feel the tears coming now that my little brother was more than likely not alive. It broke my heart to even think such a thought, but deep inside I knew it may be true. I spent the rest of the plane ride ignoring Hunter and looking out the window. I never attempted talking to him—I now liked to call him devil with curls—anymore, and he never tried to talk to me either. I was glad of it, to be completely honest. I still couldn't believe that jerk sent my little brother off with men that he knows can do very bad things to him and then tell me that he didn't even know if he's alive or not; and he even had the nerve to call him a little shit. Like, I feel bad enough as it is, why make it worse? I just decided to go to sleep, hoping to sleep through the rest of the flight.

* * *

"Wake up, we're here," I heard an annoyed voice said.

Oh it must be Hunter's, I thought. I opened my eyes and sure enough they're met with the devil himself.

"Get up, we're leaving," I did as I was told, unbuckling my seatbelt.

"How are we getting to your place?" I asked, looking around a field quit like the one where we boarded the plane.

"One of my close friends are coming to pick us up," He replied, not even looking my way.

"Oh," I simply said.

We waited for about ten minutes before a big black car with tinted windows pulled up beside us.

"Lane!" Hunter mused as the so called Lane rolled down his window. He was very attractive, if I do say so myself.

"Hunter! And who's this pretty little lady?" Lane asked, looking up and down at me.

I wanted to gouge his eyes out even though he is pretty damn hot.

"This is Cassie. She'll be working at the warehouse with us," he said evilly, grinning at me.

What did he mean by warehouse? I'm not working at some dirty warehouse.

"Oh I see, well she should fit in just fine." He smirked.

Lane got out and helped with the bags, putting them in the trunk of the SUV, while I sat in the car still wondering about that warehouse. Seconds later, Lane and Hunter jumped in the car and we drove off.

I didn't speak a word the whole time. I was a bit tired even though I did sleep pretty much the entire plane ride. Lane drove for probably an hour before we pulled up at the warehouse. There were at least a hundred cars parked outside. What in the world could be going on in there for that many cars to be out here?

Hunter took my hand and led me towards the door, while Lane followed close behind, smiling at me. It was kind of weird. I really just wanted to make a run for it but my curiosity got the best of me. As we neared the building door, music could be heard and the smell of alcohol wafted in the air. I scrunched my nose up in disgust at the strong smell.

As Hunter opened the door for me, I said a quiet thank you and went through. Once I was in the building and I have taken in my surroundings, I could already feel the tears and the need to vomit at the scene playing in front of me.

Chapter 25

Ben

I could feel the blood pumping through my veins as I was running towards the fence.

I took in sharp breaths as I run as fast as my legs would take me. I had to get to out of this field. I must get back to Mom, Dad, and Cassandra. I couldn't let these men catch me or I'm done. I picked up my speed as I heard my name being cursed in the cold night air. I started to see a light coming from behind me and began to panic. They're going to find me, I know they are. But I just couldn't let them. I turned my head around just enough to see where the light was coming from. Logan, I think his name is, had a flashlight and was scanning the field with it.

"Come on, kid, I don't have all day!" he yelled, anger laced in his words.

I began to panic even more as his voice was dangerously close to where I was at. I quickly started running faster towards the fence. They couldn't catch me. I didn't know what they would do

to me this time. I had to get back to Cassandra and protect her from that psycho man. I couldn't let him hurt her anymore. I was all she had.

I continue to run even though my legs felt like they're on fire from the bullet Hunter shot into my leg. Nate tried to get it out but I was pretty sure he just made it worse. All he did was take a knife and dug it in my leg. I thought I might die. I actually prayed to God that he would just end it now, but I guess he had better plans in mind for I'm still somehow alive. I was very thankful when I passed out while he tried to fish the bullet out of my thigh. But when I woke up, it was still there and my leg was on fire similar to the pain I'm feeling now.

I still pushed forward even though the pain was almost unbearable. I knew I had to get back to Cassie.

"Come out, come out," I heard a devilish voice sing.

I stopped dead in my tracks, not moving a muscle. I heard the sound of footsteps making their way closer to me, I didn't see the flashlight though. He must have turned it off. I quietly jogged over to a nearby tree and hid behind it.

"Come on, Logan. Let's just go back. He's obviously not going to come out." I heard Nate try to convince Logan to go back to the warehouse.

"Oh, shut the hell up! We're going to find him," He yelled at his friend.

My breathing began to quicken at the thought of them not leaving till I'm back in their arms. I sank down to the ground, trying to make myself invisible as much as possible, praying to God they don't find my hiding spot. The footsteps started to fade away, giving me hope that they're just going to go look somewhere else. I looked around the big tree where I was currently hiding behind, trying to see if I there was any sign of them. Once the coast was clear, I stood up from my sitting position and took off running towards the fence that's only fifteen feet away.

When I was only few feet away, I felt a pair of strong arms grabbed me by the waist. I started screaming but there's no hope. We're out in the middle of nowhere. I felt tears began to fall as the strong arms started to carry me back to the warehouse.

"You're going to regret running from us kid." Logan snarled and threw me over his shoulder.

* * *

I felt my body hit the floor as Logan threw me down. I hit the concrete flooring hard, making me cry out in pain.

Logan got down to my level. "Now which weapon should I use." Logan smiled evilly as he pulled out a gun and a pocket knife.

I shook my head at him as tears filled my blue eyes. He put his hand on my thigh, pushing on the bullet wound, making me wince in pain.

"Oh, does that hurt?" he asked, knowing that in fact that it did hurt.

"Y-yes," I croaked out.

"Well too bad!" he yelled in my face.

He held his knife in front of my face and slowly started to dig into my now throbbing thigh. I screamed in pain, letting the tears flow. He just laughed evilly at the pain I was going through. He raised the knife up before jamming it back into my leg. I screamed so loud I thought my lungs might burst.

Blood began to pour out of the wound as he took the now crimson red object out of my thigh. Blood started to surround the spot where I was sitting, and I started to feel light headed at the loss of blood; but I managed to get out a couple of last words before I entered a world of darkness. "You monster! I hope you die!" And those were my last words before I slowly started to slip away from the cruel world.

Chapter 26

Cassandra

My heart stopped at the scene in front of me. It was not what you would expect to see in a warehouse'.

I didn't know why I was here or my purpose here, but I sure didn't want to find out. I felt someone's breath fanned my neck before the warm air reached my ear, whispering, "Welcome home, baby girl." Hunter's deep voice growled in my ear.

This was no home, it wasn't even close to being one. There's no way I could stay here. The dim lighting and blaring music was enough to give anyone a headache.

Hunter pushed me forward into the mess of people. Some were sitting down at tables as girls gave the men lap dances, while others were on some kind of stage moving their bodies in sexual ways to hopefully turn on the men gazing at the view of their bodies that weren't very clothed. I cringed in disgust at the sight, but that wasn't what made me want to shed the tears I'd been trying to hold in. In the past few hours I could hear the sound of cries in the far-right corner of the place.

I followed the cries. Hunter was following close behind along with Lane. After pushing through drunken men and half naked girls, I was finally standing before where the cries were coming from. People gathered, surrounding the large metal cage that sits in the corner, as a girl no older than me sat in the farthest corner of the cage, curled up with no clothes on. She was trying her best to cover her body as men whistled and laughed at her. A man stood up on the metal cage, stepped over the gate part, and walked over to the young girl. Once he was standing before her, he turned to the drunken crowd.

"As I stand before you, my customers and baby girls, I would like to show all the baby girls what happens when you upset or anger our lovely customers we have here at Warehouse 17." He turned to the young shivering girl.

"What is your name dear?"

"M-Mia." She stuttered, looking down at the ground.

"Now, Mia, do you know what you have done?"

"N-no! I've done nothing!" She finally raised her voice, looking up at the man standing before her.

He stepped back, a bit shocked at her outburst towards him.

"Well, there you are wrong." He breathed.

"You haven't satisfied our customers nor have you made Warehouse 17 any money off of your ugly ass! And for that you will be punished," he hissed in her face.

"No," she said bravely, looking back at the heavy set man who wore a cowboy hat.

"No will never be an answer to me," he ordered. I'd heard that before, in fact, I was told the exact same thing by Hunter, the devil himself.

"And now it's time to teach a baby girl her lesson." At his words the crowd cheered the man as he pulled out a leather whip and turned back to the crowd, holding it up above his head saying, "Are all my baby girls watching?" He evilly grinned as the crowd went wild.

He swiftly turned around, lashing the girl. She cried in pain as deep red cuts slowly started to cover her bare body. Her screams of help only got louder and louder before I just couldn't handle it anymore. I turned to Hunter to see his reaction. His face was straight as he watched the horrific scene play before him. The cries of help started to turn into cries of defeat as I looked back at the young girl who lay lifeless on the ground in front of the man that was lashing out at her. A tear escaped, running down my right cheek. The heavy man turned to the crowd. "Now, I know she's not much now, but who would like to take Mia to bed? I know for sure you shouldn't have any trouble with her now." The devilish grin gave away what he meant.

Seconds later two guys jumped over the gate and ran to the young and beaten girl, picking her up and taking her off to only God knows where.

I turned away as the crowd started to walk away since the show was over, but before I could even take three steps someone stopped me.

"Hello, little missy." I know that country accent anywhere after what just happened. I slowly turned around to face him.

"Hi," I said quite coldly.

"This is Cassandra," Hunter told the man.

"Well it's nice to meet you. I'm Phil."

"Cassandra is going to be our latest baby girl." Hunter said quite proudly.

"Oh I see. Well a pretty face like her should fit right in here." Phil leaned in to me, whispering into my ear, "I can't wait to see you in your costume." His raspy voice spoke close to my face, too close.

"You're a disgusting big—!" I raised my voice at him only to almost get my face slapped off, not by him though. I turned my face to where the hit came from only to see a fuming Hunter.

"I see we're going to have to keep this one under control," Phil spoke with a chuckle.

"Take her away, Stiles, I'm tired of looking at her." He spat and with that, Hunter grabbed my arm, dragging me through the massive crowd of drunks.

Lane must have went somewhere else for he wasn't behind Hunter when he opened a door that was right off the hallway. We just walked down and when we got to the room, he threw me in the room. I landed on the floor, my face almost hitting the hardwood.

"What the hell was that?" he screamed, storming over to me.

Chapter 27

I quickly stood up before he could reach me and held my ground. He looked shocked that I stood to my feet instead of staying on the ground.

"Do you even know who you just said that to?" he asked, screaming in my face.

"How the hell would I know?" I screamed back.

"Don't you even use that tone with me!" he ordered, raising his hand to slap me, but I dodged the hit and run over to the other side of the room.

When I turned to look at him. He was fuming, his nostrils flared and his face turned red.

"Get. Your. Ass. Over. Here."

I pushed my luck and for once stood up for myself.

"No," I said with confidence.

He looked furious, but I could care less, he had hurt me and my family so much and I'm done doing whatever he tells me.

"No will never be an answer to me—"

I cut him off. "No." I smirked. He stormed towards me.

"You're going to wish you never said that." I walked to him before he could get to me and raised my fist, making it hit his left cheek.

He turned his face and then slowly turned to look back at me. He smacked the side of my face but I didn't care because I got to hit him first. I might regret it later but right now it felt pretty damn good.

"Try that again," he said, staring me down.

"Gladly." I smiled, hitting him again.

"You're such a bitch!"

I was pushed to the ground.

"I'd rather be a bitch than be the devil!" I screamed at him with tear-filled eyes.

He stopped dead in his tracks, freezing to the spot where he stood.

"You're a monster, Hunter, you're the devil!" I screamed, tears streaming down my face.

"No! I'm not! You don't know me!" His words sound pained as they left his mouth.

"But you are," I quietly spoke, and slowly looked at him.

We locked gazes and I swear I saw tears fill his eyes, but he quickly turned away from me.

"Get up, you need to start getting ready," he said, walking towards the door.

I sat there shocked that he didn't try to knock my face off again. I really thought he would have at least yelled at me again for talking back.

He stopped at the door, not turning around, and simply ordered, "Now." With that, I got up and walked over to where he was standing. He opened the door, letting me go first. I thought about making a run for it, but before I could, I felt a tight grip around my right wrist.

"Don't even think about it," he said with no emotion in his voice.

He led me down a hallway. We made a few turn before we stood in front of a door that reads "Baby Girls". I wondered why he's bringing me here. He then opened the door for me.

Inside, there were tables with mirrors running up against the two longest walls. Girls sit at the tables, applying makeup and putting on wigs or curling their hair to perfection. At the back wall, racks of clothes—or so called clothes— in all different colors, mostly red though, were on the hangers.

"Hi, you must be Cassandra," a deep voice spoke.

I looked to where the voice was coming from and saw a man with jet black hair and dark eyes standing in front of me, smiling.

"Yeah, I am," I said, coming off a bit cold; but still, why should I be nice? It's not like anybody in here was going to help me get home. They're all disgusting pigs who only want sex.

"Well I'm Zach." He introduced himself.

"I've heard a lot about you."

Oh great, now what did Hunter do? "Oh, good or bad?"

"Well I heard that you called Phil a disgusting pig. But I also heard that you are very beautiful which is very true." He smiled.

He has a very nice smile, well actually, he has a very nice everything. Like damn, that face and those cheekbones.

"Oh, well, thank you." I blushed. God, I'm making a fool of myself in front of a very hot man who just called me beautiful.

"Well I guess I'll let you take her from here," Hunter said awkwardly as I and Zach locked gazes.

"Yes, I'll have her ready as soon as I can," he said.

Hunter walked out of the room, leaving me with Zach.

"Well, just follow me and we'll get your hair and makeup done!"

He led me towards an empty chair. I sat down, looking at my reflection in the mirror. I saw a broken and beaten girl. My left cheek had a bruise covering most of the area. Under my eyes, dark circles were noticeable and my hair was a mess. I had no idea how Zach lied so well about me being beautiful.

"Alright, let's cover that bruise," He said, smiling. He got out some foundation and applied it to my face after washing it off with a damp cloth.

"So, when did you get the purple hair?" he asked, putting something under my eyes. I'm guessing that was to make the dark circles less noticeable.

"A few days ago. Hunter got his done too," I said, trying not to bring Hunter in this conversion. But I had a feeling he would be brought into this anyways.

"Well, I like it a lot," he said, smiling at me through the mirror.

He then got some black eyeshadow and eyeliner After he put them on, he moved on to mascara.

"I actually think we'll put fake lashes on you." After about five minutes, they were put on; and lastly he applied a red lipstick.

"Makeup is done!" He happily cheered.

"Now just for the hair."

After twenty minutes of curling my hair, he was finally done. He stepped away from my chair in front of me to let me see myself.

My mouth dropped at the sight. It didn't even look like me at all. I brought my hand up to my face and felt it to see if it was really me.

"Do you like?" Zach asked, looking at me through the mirror.

"Yes, thank you," I said, turning to him.

"Alright, well you only need your costume then I can give you back to Hunter."

I stopped and stared at him. He isn't really going to give me back to that man, is he?

"H-Hunter?" I stuttered.

"Yes. Something wrong?"

Everything was wrong. I couldn't go back to him. I was scared to know what he might do to me, I think.

"No, I guess not."

After that, he walked over to the rack and looked through all the garments before finally picking one out and giving it to me. He led me to a bathroom to put it on. I locked the door behind me and stripped down from my clothes, putting on the red garment. It was kind of made like a one-piece bathing suit but it had a skirt that went up to my ass. At least it covered my "areas." I walked out to see Zach standing before me, holding a pair of black heels. Great, heels, something that I never could walk in. He handed them to me and I sat down on a nearby chair and slipped them on slowly, standing to my feet.

"Ready?" Zach asked.

I nodded my head and he grabbed my hand and led me out of the dressing room. He then walked me down the hallway where Hunter walked me down to get to the room we just left. After about five minutes of walking, we finally stopped at a door, not the same one where I hit Hunter though. Zach knocked on the door then turned to me. "Good luck, baby girl," he said, then gently kissed my cheek, leaving me standing there staring at the plain-wooded door before it slowly opened to show Hunter.

Chapter 28

Hunter stood before me, looking me up and down, checking out the sexy garment that Zach had picked out for me. But the look on his face wasn't one you would expect to see on a man that's standing before a girl wearing lingerie. He looked... guilty? But why? Hunter didn't feel guilty, he'd done so much to me and never felt guilty before. So why would he feel guilty now?

"Uh... Come on in," he said, not sounding too sure about what he had said.

I went on in as he opened the door for me. When I was standing in the room, I let out a gasp at who was sitting on a nearby bed. Mia, the girl that had gotten beaten was sitting with her head in her hands. Quiet sobs were leaving her lips as her body trembled. The deep red cuts were obviously still visible on her pale skin. I felt someone's presence behind me as a breath fanned the side of my neck.

"Help her." His voice sounded pained.

I turned around to look at him only to see a very sad and guilty man staring back at me. Who is this Hunter? And why does he want me to help this girl?

"Please." His voice begged me.

"Okay," I agreed, walking towards her.

"Mia," I softly asked.

She looked up from her hands, staring at me with stained cheeks and bloodshot eyes from crying so much.

"I'm going to help clean up your cuts."

She nodded, taking my hand as I helped her stand to her feet. She was shaking so bad it was hard for her to keep her balance.

I looked at Hunter and asked, "Where's the bathroom?"

"Over there." He pointed to a closed door about ten feet away.

"Okay, thank you."

I carefully walked Mia towards the door, opening it to be met with a small white bathroom. I led her to sit on the toilet so I could clean her wounds. I heard a creak at the door to see Hunter standing there, staring at me.

"The first aid kit is under the sink," he told me, motioning to the cabinet under the faucet.

"Okay, thank you," I replied, opening the cabinet.

After looking for a minute, I finally found what I was looking for. I took out the peroxide, grabbed a cotton ball, and poured some on it.

"This may hurt a little bit," I say to Mia, knowing that in fact it would hurt a lot.

She nodded. I started to rub gently on a wound on her leg. She winced in pain, closing her eyes.

"I'm sorry," I spoke, feeling guilty for causing her even more pain than she was already in.

"I-It's okay," She stuttered as I brushed the cotton swab over another wounded area.

After several minutes of cleaning her cuts, I was finally done. I grabbed some kind of cloth that was in the first aid kit and started to wrap all of her wounds with it.

"There. I'm all done!" I happily cheered, standing.

"Thank you," she said.

"You didn't have to do that."

I smiled at her, saying, "It's okay, I wanted to."

She got up from where she was sitting, told me thank you again, then she left, leaving me alone with Hunter again.

I stood awkwardly in the middle of the room, staring at the floor not really knowing what to do.

"Thank you for helping Mia." Harry's raspy voice broke the silence.

"Mia's brother is a dear friend of mine and I just couldn't watch her in pain for any longer. He told me to watch after her," he explained to me, staring at me from his sitting position on the bed.

"Well you're welcome, but it was really nothing. You could've done it yourself," I said back, not making eye contact.

"That's the thing, Mia is afraid of me so there's no way she would have let me." I nodded, understanding why Mia would be afraid of him. Heck, I'm still kind of afraid of him.

"So, um... Where am I sleeping?" I asked.

"With me," he simply said.

Chapter 29

The words were playing over in my head so much that I didn't even realize that Hunter had said something else to me.

"W-what?" I asked, snapping out of my thoughts of having to share a bed, yet again, with Hunter.

"I said, but first let's get you changed. You don't look very comfortable in that, whatever that is you're wearing."

I was relieved to get the sexy garment off, but I was also nervous to know what I would be putting on next.

Hunter walked over to a dresser, opening the top drawer and digging around till he pulled out a piece of clothing. He then opened the drawer below the one he had just looked through and took out yet another piece of fabric. I stood awkwardly in the middle of the room as he walked back to where I'm standing.

"Here, put these on," he said, handing me a pair of boxers and a black t-shirt.

I took them from him and walked to the bathroom, locking the door behind me. I turned to the mirror to have one last look at the sexy garment. I still couldn't believe I put this thing on. It's way out of my comfort zone. It's way too tight for one thing, like I could barely breathe; and since I was too big for it, my breasts were trying to pop out of the top. The so cold skirt was so short I could barely even walk without showing my ass.

After giving the sexy garment one last disgusted look, I stripped from the clothing, leaving it to pool at my feet. I looked down at my feet to see I was still wearing the damn heels Zach picked out for me. I slipped out of the uncomfortable shoes, kicking them over to the side as I pulled the boxers up and held the top up with the statement "Rolling Stones" in the front. It has a few holes in it but it would be fine since all I'd be doing is sleeping in it.

Once done, I looked through the cabinets, hoping to find a washed cloth of some sort. There seemed to be everything but washed cloths in the small cabinet under the sink. All I could seem to find was shaving cream, razors, and cleaning supplies. I stood to my feet, defeated. I walked over to the bathroom door, first picking up my clothes off the ground before unlocking the door and turning the light off. Hunter was sitting on the bed, reading a book. I stood at the door.

"Hunter?" I asked.

He brought his attention away from the book and to my face. "Yeah?"

"Do you have any washed cloths? I really need to wash this makeup off," I explained leaning against the door frame.

He stood to his feet, saying, "Yeah, they're under the cabinet—"

"I looked, they're not there," I sa5d, cutting him off before he could finish.

"Oh, well I thought I put some under there." He breathed out, scratching the back of his neck.

"I guess not." I awkwardly laugh. Why did it get so awkward?

"Do you by any chance know where some more are?" I asked, hoping he would just find me a washed cloth so I could go to bed.

"Here, let me look in the bathroom, maybe I'll find one." With that he walked over to me, eyeing his shirt that I was wearing.

I moved out of the way so he could go into the restroom.

"Shirt looks good on you," he complimented, not making eye contact with me as he opened a small closet I must have not known was there.

"Oh. Uh, thanks," I awkwardly replied.

He dug around for a minute before he finally found a wash cloth.

"Here you go," he said, handing me the blue-colored cloth.

"Thanks."

"You're welcome." He left me in the bathroom to wash my face. I turned on the faucet, getting the little towel wet.

Hunter, sure, was acting weird. Like, he's being oddly nice and not demanding like he normally is. Maybe Hunter does have a nice side. Eh, probably not, he must think he's going to get "some" from me tonight. Well boy, he is wrong.

After I was done washing my face and all the makeup was off, I had totally forgot about a toothbrush. I really wished someone would have brought in my suitcase. I could really use it.

I walked, out deciding I could go one night without brushing my teeth. Hunter was again sitting on the bed, reading some kind of book. I walked over to him.

"What are you reading?"

He looked up from the book and said, "Thought I might give it a try." He was holding up the book to where I can read the title *The Holy Bible*. I think it is pretty odd but hey, it ain't my place to judge.

"I think it's actually just a bunch of bullshit though," he said, closing the book and laying it beside him.

"Like, it says that God is a loving and kind God who loves everyone. But if that's so true then why would he let people die in awful ways or why do some people have better lives than others?" I sat there taking in what he's saying.

I was raised in a church so it was hard for me to hear him call something that I strongly believe in to be just a bunch of bullshit. I guess it was hard for him to believe in something that sounded impossible though, but the words themselves say, "I'm possible."

"Hunter, God gives the strongest people the hardest lives, and God is a loving God. Earth is only our temporary home. One day when we die, I believe and many others do as well that those who believe in God will live forever in Heaven and those who don't will sadly burn in Hell for the rest of eternity."

He looked at me with saddened eyes.

"It's too late for me. I lost God when He took my mother away." And with that he got up and left the room.

I was not really sure where he went but I guess he just needed some time. I sat back on the bed, wondering where life was taking me. I thought about making a run for it, but before Hunter left I heard the clicking of the lock. I got under the covers and pulled the blankets close to my face and slowly started to drift off to sleep.

* * *

I woke up to the closing of a door and the sound of footsteps. I rolled over to my side to see Hunter getting in bed. He pulled the covers up to his armpits then reached over to the nightstand, grabbing what looked like a lighter. A few seconds later, he lighted it and started taking long drags of it. Within minutes of him smoking, I started to cough from my asthma. It always acted up when I'm around smokers. I waited a few minutes, hoping I would be able to stand him smoking, but it wasn't working very well.

"Is there any way you could not do that in here?" I asked, afraid I might anger him.

I knew whenever my mother would try and tell a smoker at a restaurant to stop smoking because she knew it messed with my asthma, they would always get mad and just keep smoking.

"Why? Does it bother you?" he asked, turning to face me.

"Yes it does. I have asthma..." I trailed off.

He turned back to look up at the ceiling and let out a small chuckle.

"I have asthma as well." He laughed.

"But doesn't that really bother it?"

"Yeah it does, but it's worth it." With that, he put the cigarette out and turned to face me.

"So tell me about yourself," He randomly asked.

I thought it was a bit weird that he actually wanted to know, but oh well, I would tell him.

"Uh, I'm kind of a boring person to be completely honest," I saied, trying to think of something that might interest him.

"What do you want to become in life? Like, what's your dream job?"

I knew exactly what I wanted to be but I wasn't really sure how he would react to it.

"I, uh... I want to be a therapist," I admitted.

He scrunched his eyebrows together and said, "That's a horrible job."

I was taken aback by his words. Why would he say it's a horrible job?

"How so?" I sat up a bit more so I could look down at him.

"It's a horrible job because whoever you're talking with will hate you. Nobody likes going to a therapist." He breathed out.

He was right about that. Nobody ever liked going to the therapist. Heck, I didn't even like going. I was made to go when I was 15. I had problems with making friends and just overall fitting in. My only friends back then were Summer and Jackie, but even then I sometimes wondered if they were truly my friends. I mean we would hang out and do things together, but I kind of felt like they just felt sorry for me. Two months after my fifteenth birthday, Jackie was in a car wreck. She had just gotten her license not even a month before the wreck. She was driving on a country road and wasn't paying attention. A semi-truck hit her head on. I lost one of my only best friends that day. When I was told she had died at the scene, I broke down crying right there in my living room.

My father told me to toughen up because he had lost his best friend in the army. My mother tried to comfort but it just wasn't working.

After she died, life got harder. School stressed me out to the point I just wanted to die, but none of that was the reason I was sent to see a therapist. Sure it was a small part of it but the day my mother caught me with a blade was the day she scheduled an appointment to see the local therapist.

"You are right about that. Nobody likes going, but I want to help people and heal them from their past kind of like a doctor. A doctor heals people physically but I could help heal them mentally." I said, smiling at how exciting it sounded to help young men and women overcome their past or things that they're dealing with at the moment.

"I guess it would be but still, they would all hate you," Hunter said bitterly.

I exhaled sharply and replied, "Maybe not all of them."

"Yes, all of them."

"No, not all," I said, starting to get annoyed with him.

"Yes," He smiled at me.

"No."

"Yes."

"No."

"Yes!" He smirked.

"God, you are annoying." I rolled over on my side, turning away from the man who gets under my skin so very much. I then felt someone slowly rub their finger across my bare arm, sending chills running down my spine.

"I didn't mean to upset you," he rasped in my ear, his hot breath fanning my bare neck.

"I-It's jus—"

"Shh, go to sleep." And with that he wrapped his arm around my waist, pulling me into him till my back was to his front.

I slowly started to drift off to the sound of Hunter's light breathing.

* * *

I heard the sound of heavy footsteps approaching the room I was currently in. I looked over to where Hunter was sleeping only to find an empty bed. Seconds later, the door burst open to a pissed Hunter. I backed up against the bed frame as he stared at me with horror.

"You," he said, pointing one of his big fingers at me and started storming over to me.

"You told Mia to run, didn't you?" he yelled, grabbing my feet and pulling me out of the bed.

I landed on the cold, hard ground with a thud.

"Didn't you?" he screamed in my face.

Tears poured out of my eyes, making my sight blurry.

"N-no, I d-didn't," I said, pushing myself up against the wall nearby.

"Don't lie to me!" Hunter grabbed my arms, picking me up and throwing me over his shoulder.

"I didn't say anything, I swear!" I yelled, hitting him on the back as he stormed out of his room.

"You're going to wish you hadn't," he told me evilly.

I screamed and cried out for help, hoping someone would make this psycho let me go; but all the people we passed just stared and walked on by, not giving the girl on the crazy man's back a second thought. Hunter opened a big door which was followed by him walking downstairs. It got colder and darker the farther he went. All that could be heard was the sound of my heavy breathing and the sound of my beating heart which I'm pretty sure Hunter could hear. All of a sudden, he stopped walking and pulled out a pair of keys. He picked one out, stuck it in the lock and opened the big door. The room was dimly lit, making it hard to see. He threw me on the cold ground, telling me, "Next time you'll think before you speak." With that he left the room, locking the door behind him.

I quietly stood to my feet, running over to the metal door, pushing and shoving on it hoping for it to let me out. I screamed at Hunter as I saw him walk up the stairs, followed by the sound of the door being slammed shut. I stood at the door, sobbing, trying my best to stop crying; but I couldn't until a sweet little sounding voice asked, "Will you play dolls with me?"

Chapter 30

I froze at the sound of the voice. Everything suddenly went dead quite.

My breathing had completely stopped. The only sound was the small droplets of water, dripping from the concrete ceiling onto the cold floor where I stood. I took a deep breath, telling myself it was just my mind playing tricks on me as I turned around slowly, not in any rush, to see what could possibly be standing before me. I squinted from the dimly lit room as I saw an outline of a small figure slowly walking towards me. I took a step back, holding my breath as the person neared closer to me.

"I asked you a question." The same sweet voice spoke now, standing where the light falls over her face.

It was a young girl, no older than seven with curly, dirty blonde hair that cascades down the front of her whitish brown dress. The dress she wore went down to her ankles with holes covering the bottom of it. But that's not really what scared me most about her. One side of her pale faced skin looked as if it had been burned. There were even places in her dress that has holes, I'm guessing from some kind of fire.

"Are you alright?" she asked, coming even closer.

I took a step back only for my back to hit the cold metal door.

"I-I…" I couldn't even form words as I stared at the young girl.

She looked like something out of a horror film, one which I would not watch. Is this a joke? Is Hunter just trying to scare me? Or is this actually happening? I didn't know and that's what scared me.

"I would really like for you to play dolls with me. It's been so long since anybody has come to visit me." Her sweet voice made her even creepier.

"I won't hurt you, I promise." She was practically begging me to play with her, but I just couldn't bring myself to do so.

I mean, this isn't normal, a little girl being locked up in a basement for who knows how long. Why would anybody do this? She's just a little girl, a creepy one at that, but still.

"You know, it's rude not to speak when you are spoken to." It sounded like something my mother would tell me when I was little.

"My mommy always told me that." So her mother would tell her that too.

I took a few deep breaths, knowing I'd have to talk to the young girl at some point, considering it didn't look like I was getting out of here anytime soon.

"Sure, I'll play, but first what's your name?" I asked, trying my best not to stutter and sound afraid of the young girl, which I am very much.

"I can't tell you that," she answered, swaying back and forth.

"And why not?" I raised a brow.

"Because mommy always said don't tell a stranger your name, age, or address." she said matter-of-factly.

"Well didn't your mommy tell you not to talk to strangers?" I asked taking a step near her.

"I know my mommy always did." I childishly spoke.

"Well my mommy said you can talk to strangers as long as you don't tell them your name, age, or address." She spoke, putting her hands on her hips.

I thought for a minute. How could I convince her to tell me her name or at least something about herself?

"I'll tell you my name if you tell me yours," I bribed.

She looked down at her feet. I guessed she was trying to decide if she really wanted to tell me or not. After a few more seconds passed, she finally looked up from her stare at the cold, wet ground.

"No. It's a secret," she said, smiling at me from across the room. It was a creepy smile in fact.

"You never answered my question." She took small steps towards me.

I stood my ground, knowing there was nowhere I could go. I thought of the choices I have. I could either scream, hoping that maybe someone will happen to hear me and come rescue me from this demon child, or just play damn dolls with her. She stared at me, well more like through me!

"I'll play but can I be Ken?" I asked playfully, hoping to break the awkward mood that seemed to lurk in the air.

She looked at me as if I've killed someone.

"There is no Ken," she said with all seriousness.

"I ripped his head off," she finished, smiling at the thought of her cruel actions upon the toy doll.

"Why would you do that?" I was afraid of what made her rip the poor doll's head off.

She stopped moving completely and looked me dead in the eyes as a small tear ran down her cheek. "A boy once broke my heart. In ways you probably will never understand." She's speaking beyond her years.

"You're like seven. How could a boy break your heart?" I wondered, truly wanting to know the answer.

"Like I said, you wouldn't understand." She turned away from me and walked over to a corner, bending over and picking something up.

I couldn't quite tell what she picked up before she started walking back over to me.

"Who do you want to play as?" she asked, holding up two dolls.

One had brown hair and green eyes, while the other one had reddish brown hair with grey eyes. They both looked sad. But how? They are just dolls.

"What are their names?" I asked, wondering if they even had any.

"This is Annie," she said, holding up the doll with green eyes.

"And this one is Mia," she happily spoke, handing me the doll with grey eyes.

I took it from her examining the doll. I had heard the name before. Well actually, I had just had the name screamed at me not long ago, but I pushed the thought to the back of my mind as the little nameless girl spoke again.

"What's your name?" she asked, sitting down on the ground.

"Cassandra," I answered, taking a seat on the ground as well even though it was wet from the dripping ceiling.

We played with the dolls for probably two hours, she just kept asking loads of questions and me giving in to answering them. I tried asking her questions but most of them she wouldn't answer and just said, "Mommy told me not to tell strangers that." It got on my nerves because by the time she had asked half of her questions, I wasn't considered a stranger anymore. But I did found out her favorite color. It's green.

She was now lying down on a bed in the far-right corner of the room while I sat by the metal door, praying to God that somehow I'll get out of this mess. I closed my eyes, hoping to escape the world.

* * *

I woke up to the sound of a doorknob being twisted and the cold door slowly being pushed open, jerking my body forward. I got out of the way and jumped up to my feet in hopes of a rescue. When the door was fully open, Zach, my stylist (as if I would dare call him that), stod before me.

"Zach?" I asked.

"Yeah, it's me." He replied with a smile.

"What are you doing down here?" I asked aloud while taking a step closer to the beautiful man.

"I came to warn you," He breathed out.

"Of what?"

"Hunter. He's going to be down here soon, and he didn't seem very happy at all when I saw him a few moments ago—" Before he could finish what he was about to say, footsteps could be heard marching down the stairs.

A few seconds later, the devil himself stood in front of us, breathing heavily.

"Get over here now," he spoke sternly, his eyes burning holes through me.

Zach stepped in front of me, shielding me somewhat from the raging man standing before us.

"I think you should leave, Hunter—"

"Shut the hell up and move, you little piece of shit," he said, stepping closer to us.

"No." Zach bravely stood up for the both of us.

"What did you just say?" Hunter asked, cocking his head to the side.

"I said no—" Before I could comprehend what was happening, Hunter had Zach pinned to the ground, smashing his face over and over.

I threw my hands over my mouth as a gasped left my lips.

"Hunter, stop!" I yelled at him and tried to stop him by repeatedly, pulling on his bicep.

He just shoved me to the ground and I landed on my butt. I heard some sniffling over to my right only to find the little girl walking towards me with tears in her eyes.

"Go back over there, sweetie," I commanded.

She just stood there, frozen on the spot, and just stared at the scene in front of her. I looked back to the two boys only to find one one of them (Zach, to be more specific) on the ground, while Hunter was on his feet, breathing heavily. He slowly turned to face me and said, "Get up now." I didn't move a muscle at his words. I just sat there, staring blankly at him.

"Now!" He ordered, his voice echoing through the dark basement.

I was unable to move as I stared at the blood oozing out of Zach's body. I could only hope he was still alive. I wouldn't know what to do without him. Even though I barely knew him, it would still hurt to see him gone considering he is the only person here that had been nice to me.

"Fine! Ifou don't want to get up, I'll make you!" Hunter screamed and marched over to me.

He grabbed my arm, pulled me up from the cold ground, and threw me over his shoulder.

"No! Let me go!" I screamed at him, hitting his back.

"I can't do that, baby girl. After all, there're men waiting for you."

I cringed at the nickname.

"I'd rather die!" I yelled at him.

He stopped dead in his tracks and set me back down on the ground, but still held on to me with a firm grip.

"You what?" he asked without giving away any emotion.

"I said, I'd rather die." A smirk started to form on his hard features right before he spoke four simple yet deadly words.

"That can be arranged."

He grabbed me again threw me over his shoulder before I could even say anything, and stalked back to the room he had just left. He threw me against the cold wall, pushed his body onto mine, and smirked while doing so. It was obvious he enjoyed this. He put his hand in his back pocket and pulled out a pair of handcuffs. *Not this again*, I thought. I tried struggling, but he still managed to loop the cuffs on a bar, about four feet above my head, on the wall, then strapped both my wrists onto them, thereby cuffing my hands over my head. Once he released me, I was dangling in the air, my feet almost touching the ground.

"Don't mess with me, Cassie." He turned away from me and headed towards Zach, picking him up then doing the same to him.

As Hunter walked out of the room, he looked back at the little girl standing alone in the corner of the room and stared at her with such guilt; but he quietly turned away from her, stalked out and locked the door behind him.

All that went through my head was that we're going to die.

Chapter 31

It's been twenty minutes since Hunter stormed out, which left me and Zach hanging on the wall by handcuffs. I still couldn't believe he did that. Yes, I know I said I would rather die, but I didn't think this would be the way he would chose to do it.

I heard a sniffle coming from a corner in the room. I looked towards the direction of the noise to find the little girl staring blankly at the door as tears ran down her cheeks.

"Sweetie, what's wrong?" I asked., The nickname didn't suit her by any means but heck, I didn't know what else to call her.

She didn't even budge, not one bit, so I tried again. "What's wrong? Say something," I encouraged, but she still didn't move.

It was like she was in shock or something. I decided to give her some time since I really couldn't do anything else, considering I was handcuffed to a wall. I directed my attention to Zach, who hung unconsciously with his head dangling between his arms, both of which were strapped together at the top by handcuffs. I could only hope he's still alive. I wouldn't know what to do if he isn't.

I knew I haven't known him for very long, but he was the only one that wasactually nice. Plus, I'm pretty sure he's the only sane man in this warehouse thing.

"Zach?" I asked, hoping he would just magically wake up. But I was almost positive he wouldn't.

I waited a minute before I tried again, "Can you hear me? Zach?"

Still nothing.

I swung my legs lightly towards his direction and hit his side, hoping it would wake him up. He seemed to stir a little but still didn't wake up.

"Now what?" I said to myself out loud, trying to think of some way to get these stupid handcuffs unlocked.

I stayed quiet, thinking to myself. What to do?

"Why did he do that?" The little girl standing on the other side of the room asked, not tearing her attention away from the steel door.

"What do you mean?" I asked, wondering what the creepy little girl had to say.

"Why did Hunter hit that boy?" she said, pointing at Zach's hanging body. "And then handcuff you both?"

I honestly didn't know what to tell her. I mean, what do I say to a seven year old? That I would rather die then let Hunter force me to have sex with a complete stranger, and so he chained me up and left me to ro? Yeah, I'm pretty sure that would be a bit too much for a seven year old to understand. I pushed the horrid thought aside and just went with, "I really have no idea why he did this."

"Is he still alive?"

I looked at him, hoping to God he was. As I looked closer, I saw his chest rising up and down lightly. I breathed a sigh of relief. "Yes, yes he is," I said, turning towards the young girl.

It was silent for a while till a thought popped into my head.

"Is there any way you might have a key for these handcuffs?" I asked, already knowing the answer will be no. But, heck, might as well try, right?

She pondered for a moment, making me wonder if maybe the creepy little girl did have them.

"No. No, I do not," she answered, shattering my hopes.

I really needed to find a way out of this hellhole.

I looked around the room, hoping to find something the little girl could hand me something that would possibly unlock these cuffs.

The only thing I saw was a twinsized bed, the two Barbie dolls, and a rocking chair. I was hoping to maybe find a fork, or anything else that's thin and sharp, so I could try picking the lock, even though I was almost positive it would fail. Suddenly, a thought popped into my head.

"Hey, little girl," I called out.

"Yes?" she answered.

"Do you happen to have a bobby pin?" She thought for a moment then started to comb through her hair till she pulled one out.

"Here you go," she said, walked over to me, and held the pin up in the air.

I don't think she realized that I can't get it from her.

"No, no, sweetie. I need you to do something for me, alright?"

She shot me a confused look with one hand on her hip and said, "And what might that be?" Her head was cocked to one side.

"I need you to stick that bobby pin in that lock over there." I nodded to the big steel door across the room. "Do you think you could do that?"

"I can try," she answered, walking to the other side of the room where the door was located.

She took the pin, put it into the lock, and started to poke it around and twist the knob at the same time. After a minute of doing that, she puffed out of frustration and stomped back towards me. I never thought see someone as young as her look so pissed.

"It isn't working." She put her hands, yet again, back on her small waist. "And what exactly did you want me to do?" she asked, scrunching her eyebrows together.

"Well, I wanted you to pick the lock so the door would open."

She looked at me like I was stupid. What did I say? Did I have something on my face?

"I have a key." She smirked, sticking her small, pale hands in the pockets of her white dress. Seconds later, she pulled out a small silver key.

"How did you get that?"

"One time, a man came down here to give me Mia and Annie," she explained, pointing over to the dolls lying on, I'm guessing, her bed.

"And he left this key." As she held up the key to where I can see it, I wondered why she didn't try to escape.

"Why didn't you try to escape? After all, you have a key. So why didn't you?"

She pondered the question for a second, "I never had a reason to."

Oh, was all I was able to say.

"So, do you think you can get the key for these cuffs from Hunter?" I asked, praying to God she'd be brave enough to venture out on her own.

"Well… I don't know." She hesitated and swayed back and forth.

"You can do it. I know you can!" I encouraged.

"I guess I could try." She smiled. It was a happy smile, even though it looked creepy as hell with her face all messed up . With that, she skipped off to the other side of the room, unlocking and opening the door with ease.

I could only hope she would be alright. I hope Hunter doesn't try and hurt her. He wouldn't, would he? I can only pray that he wouldn't. And that's just what I did. I prayed, asking God to keep her safe and for me to be with Ben.

Ben.

Is he still alive? A tear rolled down my cheek. Not knowing if my own baby brother was still living or not was excruciating. Once my prayer was done, I tried my best to relax. I was almost asleep, somehow, when I heard a raspy, broken voice call my name.

Chapter 32

I turned my head towards the direction of the voice and found Zach slowly coming to. He started to mumble words I couldn't quite understand. He moved his head back and forth with his eyes still shut tightly.

"W-Where am I?" he stuttered, finally waking up enough to speak actual words.

"You're in the basement, Zach. Remember?" I asked, knowing there's a good chance he didn't remember what happened considering the hits he took from Hunter.

"B-Basement. Why the hell am I in a basement?" he yelled. I could tell he was starting to panic as he struggled to move from against his restraints on the stone wall.

"Zach, calm down. You're alright." I tried to comfort him, but it didn't work because he just kept on yanking the chains. B It was no use, he'd only enp up hurting himself if he continues to do that.

"Zach, you need to calm down. You'll only hurt yourself when you keep struggling against the chains," I said sternly, looking over at him.

He stopped what he was doing and relaxed. I let out a sigh of relief, glad that he finally stopped harming himself.

"What happened?" he asked, looking at me.

I took a deep breath and then spoke. "Hunter hit you really hard and then you blacked out," I answered.

He looked at me a bit shocked then slowly realized what had happened.

"Okay, I'm starting to remember that, but how did we get up here?" He wondered, motioning to the handcuffs.

"After you blacked out, Hunter then cuffed us to the wall," I spoke, furious at Hunter for doing this.

"That bastard," Zach said under his breath, but I heard it clearly.

I just laughed and agreed with what he had called Hunter.

"Where's that little girl?"

I looked at him and said, "She had a key to the door, so I sent her to get the keys for these stupid handcuffs," I replied while he nodded.

"Good idea."

It it was silent for what felt like an eternity before Zach finally spoke up again.

"I uh... have a question," he stammered.

"And that is?" I said, looking at him.

"Uh... Does my hair look alright?" he asked with all seriousness.

I couldn't believe he was actually worried about his hair — his hair, of all things! — when there were more important things to be worried about, such as being handcuffed to a basement wall below a whorehouse.

"You can't be serious?" I asked, raising a brow.

"Um, well I'm not joking." He laughed.

I just laughed along with him and said, "It looks fine." I smiled at him and he returned a smile as well.

"So why don't you tell me about yourself? I mean, it doesn't look like we'll be getting out of here anytime soon. Might as well take this time to get to know each other," he asked, turning his body a little so he was somewhat facing me.

"Well I'm sixteen, almost seventeen. I have a little brother named Ben, but I'm not even sure if he is still alive. Hunter sent him with some men. He told me he would let Ben go if I went with him, so, of course, I agreed. But it turns out he lied, and now I have no idea if my brother is even alive or not." I struggled to speak as the tears fell. I wasn't planning on crying in front of Zach but I guess I couldn't help myself.

"Oh, babe, I'm sorry to hear that," he spoke softly to me. "It'll all be okay. We'll get out of this and you'll find your brother and Hunter will be out of the picture for good."

I smiled at his words. Hunter being out of my life for good, how wonderful that would be? Yet when he is gone, I guess I'll just go back to my normal boring life. Yes, I know that he has done awful things to me, but the mystery behind him intrigues me. The tattoos that mark his skin, I want to know the story behind them. The scars he has scattered across his body, I want to run my fingers over them as he tells the story behind each one. I want to know his story and why he took me and Ben and I want to know him.

"We'll get out of this... together." He smiled at me, trying to reassure me that we really will.

"Thank you," I whispered to him.

"For what?"

"For giving me hope," I smiled looking up at the ceiling.

"We all need hope because without hope there is no reason to fight, and you... you have given me hope. Something to fight for." I relaxed my mind now, knowing that we would get out of this together.

"Well then, you are very welcome. I can't imagine a pretty face like yours rotting away to nothing in this hellhole."

I blushed, loving the complement from such a handsome face. I'd never seen a man quite like him. To be that beautiful and kind, he must have girls all over him back home, well, wherever back home is for him.

"Well, thank you."

"It's true, you are beautiful."

At his words, my cheeks reddened probably making me look something like a tomato.

"Somebody's blushing." He's teasing me which only made me blush even more.

"So where's home for you?" I asked, looking at him hoping my cheeks had toned down a bit.

"Somebody's changing the subject," he said in that same teasing way, dragging out the word subject.

"Nah. I'm just messing with you. I'm from Florida."

"If you're from Florida then why the British accent?" I wondered.

He laughed lightly then said, "Well I've lived here since I was nine so you kinda just pick up on it."

"Ah, I see."

"Yep, but where are you from?"

I thought back to my home in Mississippi and how boring Brettwood high school really is. The people there are just stuck-up rich kids who only like you for your money. That's probably why I never had very many friends because my family isn't poor but we're not rich either.

"Well I live in Thaxton, Mississippi and go to Brettwood High where everyone only thinks of money and sex like legit. That's all that goes on there. I once walked into the girls' bathroom to see a cheerleader and our main baseball playing, doing "it" on the floor. It was disgusting to say the least." I cringed at the memory.

Oh, that must've sucked."

I looked at him. "Yes, yes it did. But it could have been worse. One of my friends, Sara, walked in on our Math teacher doing 'it' with a student. She said and I quote, 'I've never in my life had an urge to vomit like I did after seeing my teacher's shining white ass humping a random whore from our school.' I love her to death but for the longest time, she tried to explain what pose they were trying to achieve." I admitted.

"Well that's not nasty at all." Zach awkwardly laughed. "I feel very sorry for your friend."

"I don't—She deserved it." I laughed, looking at him.

"How did she deserve it?" he asked, raising an eyebrow.

"Well let's just say she walked on me and my old boyfriend messing around when he told her not to bother us.

Flash Back

I and Sean were currently at a pool party, the loud music and screaming teens starting to give me a headache. I looked around for the pool area hoping to find Sean so he could take me home, but he's nowhere in sight. I looked in the water but still nothing.

I got up from my lawn chair, putting my towel on the back of the chair only leaving myself in my blue bikini. I walked around the house to the front yard only to find him throwing a football back and forth with some guys from school.

"Sean, over here." I called out, getting his attention. He looked at me, still holding tightly to the football. He smiled at me as I walked towards him. "What's up, babe?" he asked when I was only a few feet away.

"Can you take me home? I have a headache plus it's a bit boring sitting back there all alone," I said, pointing to the backyard where the pool is located.

"I can make it less boring." He smirked at me.

Sean is incredibly tall like 6'3 and I am only 5'5. I tell him all the time he should be on the basketball team at school, but no; he plays football.

"I don't think that would be a good idea," I said, smiling and turning to walk away from him; but he grabbed my arm and said, "I'll be back in a few, guys."

He yelled to the team and dragged me into the house. We entered the kitchen where my friend Sara was sitting at the counter, biting into a pizza. "Hey, where are you two off to?" she asked, raising a brow. "Upstairs," Sean quickly answered. "Oh, well can I come?" *Was she stupid?* I thought. "No," Sean snapped and dragged me up the stairs and into a bedroom.

As soon as the door was shut, he slammed me against the wall and started to roughly kiss all over my skin. He pulled my legs and I wrapped them around his waist only to have him lay me on the bed while he kissed my neck. I knew what he had in mind and I really didn't want to do it in a stranger's bed. I felt so exposed to him while I lay on the bed with only my bikini. His kisses started to go lower till they're in the valley of my breasts. He tried to untie my bikini top, but before he could the door opened to Sara.

"Hey, Cassandra, your mom's here—Oh shit, girl!"

* * *

"Cassandra I got it!" I heard a familiar voice say as I snapped out of my flashback. The little girl stood in front of me holding a set of keys in her small pale hands.

"Oh my God, you did it!" I said in joy.

She stood on her tippy toes to hand me the keys.

After a bit of struggling with the cuffs, I was finally free. I walked towards Zach unlocking his as well, setting him free. We both rubbed our wrists for a minute. They were terribly sore from the chain cuffs.

"Thanks," Zach said while rubbing his wrist.

"You're welcome. Now let's get out of here," I said smiling.

"That's the thing, how?"

"We can't go upstairs or we'll be caught, and there's no way out this room. So how?" he asked.

I looked around, pondering on how exactly we'd get out of this mess.

"There's a secret tunnel right over there," the creepy-yet-helpful little girl said, pointing over beside her bed.

"There is? You have got to be kidding?" I was shocked, not believing it was going to be that easy.

"Yes, there is. I'm not lying." With that, she took us over to her bed, telling Zach to move the wooden bed a bit; and that's just what he did.

After the bed was moved, I saw the tunnel the young girl was talking about. "Where does it lead to?" Zach asked, looking at the dark tunnel that leads to only God knows where. "Outside the warehouse. I think the parking lot," she replied.

"Well then let's go before someone comes down here," he said going first into the tunnel. I we second and the little girl went last. We had to go on our hands and knees to fit through the narrow space but we managed. It's a bit wet and it didn't smell the best, but I just kept telling myself it could be worse.

As we're crawling, I heard Zach joyfully say, "I see a light." I smiled waiting the moment when I finally get home and out of this hellhole. Zach crawled out first, landing onto the grass wet from the dew. Then I crawled out, standing to my feet and giving Zach a hand up as well.

"Finally. We're out!" he said breathing in the fresh outdoors.

I turned my attention to the little girl as she just sat with her feet dangling off the edge of the tunnel exit. "Come on, we gotta go." I said, holding my hand out for her to grab.

She looked up at me with hopeful green eyes. "You really don't know who I am, do you?"

I shook my head knowing I didn't.

"I'm Lily," she simply said.

I had heard the name before. Well actually I heard Hunter telling me about his sister and that she died and her name is Lily. Lily is Hunter's dead sister.

Chapter 33

I stood there in shock at what Lily had just said. She can't be. Can she? I mean there was always that little voice at the back of my head telling me something was up with this little girl, but really? Hunter's dead sister? Wait. She can't be dead, or I wouldn't be able to see her or talk to her. I snapped out of my shocked state as her voice speaks.

"Are you alright?" she asked, tilting her head to the side and cocking an eyebrow at me.

"You're supposed to be dead," I blurted out.

Zach seemed to zone back in at my words. He was leaning in towards me to hear our conversation more clearly.

"I am," she simply replied.

I stood frozen yet again at the young girl's words.

"I died in a fire on May 7, 2004," she spoke.

I stayed there in shock at her words. My birthday is May 7 and she died during it.

"I would have been turning eighteen this year if it weren't for that fire."

"Wait, so you're seventeen? That's why you act so much older."

She smiled at me saying, "You're very smart. But have you figured out why Hunter took you yet?"

I thought about her question for a moment, thinking of the endless possibilities. "I don't have a clue," I answered so she would just tell me.

"I was all Hunter had left when I died in that fire. It tore him to pieces. He just couldn't let me go."

I listened nodding my head for her to continue.

"My body still lies in the hospital a few miles from here, wasting away in a bed with a machine that's making me breath. It's been ten years. I'm ready to go home. I'm ready to die fully, Cassandra. You have to help me," she begged, tears streaming down her face.

I felt so bad for her. Even though I didn't completely understand, I understood enough to know that she was ready to go. "I will, but how does this have anything to do with me?" I asked, hopeful.

She took in a deep breath. "After a year, I think Hunter realized that I wasn't coming back so he went off and started searching for another me, someone to call his own. Someone that he could control yet still love at the same time. He had thrown multiple girls down in that dungeon, leaving them there to wonder what they had done to deserve that treatment. But of course he would never tell them why he had put them down there. After leaving them with me for weeks, he would then give them off to the men in this hellhole, letting them do whatever they wanted with them," she finished, looking right at me.

Zach's mouth had hit the ground from pure shock. "What the heck is going on?" I heard him say to himself. Then he just walked away to only God knows where.

"Cassandra, Hunter is using you as a personal Lily. As me."

"But I don't even look like you at all," I said, frustrated with this whole thing.

"I'm sorry but it's true," she sadly said. "But you still must help me, then run as far away from Hunter as you can."

I nodded, willing to do anything for her now. "What can I do?" I asked, hoping it would be something easy so I could hurry and get out of this town.

"I need you to kill me."

Her words felt like knife stabbing my heart. I couldn't just kill her like it was nothing then go on with my daily life.

"I-I can't," I stuttered.

"You must though."

"Set me free, let me go home."

I nodded, agreeing to the horrible deal.

After she gave me directions to the hospital and what room she was in, we were saying our goodbyes.

"I'll miss you even if I hardly got to know you," she mumbles on my shoulder.

"I'll miss you too," I whispered back, pulling away from the embrace.

"Thank you again. But remember after the job is done, don't look back. Forget about Hunter. Go home, find your brother, and live a happy life." She smiled, getting back in the tunnel.

"I will, but I sadly know that my brother is no longer in this world," I spoke back, letting a tear stream down my cheek.

She turned to me and said, "You are sadly wrong. He is still living." She grinned at me, making my world light up at the thought of my brother not dead.

But I had to ask. "How do you know?"

"I can feel it," she yelled back as she disappeared inside the tunnel.

With that, I grabbed Zach and told him the directions to the hospital. We got into his big black SUV and drive down the narrow, graveled drive. I looked back at the warehouse, knowing deep in my heart that I am doing the right thing and that I will never have to worry about Hunter again.

Chapter 34

We were just now getting onto the main road on our way to the hospital where Lily is. I still couldn't believe I agreed to do this. In a way, I feel like I'm doing the right thing because she has been there for ten years; but then again, I feel like a horrible person because I'm killing an innocent child. I would have never agreed to it if she didn't personally ask me to.

"Okay, please tell me what the hell is going on?" Zach asked, looking nervous from the driver's side.

"To be honest, I really don't know." I sighed, shifting in my seat to get comfortable.

"Well then, why exactly are we going to a hospital to see a half-dead girl?"

I thought about it for a second, asking myself if I should really tell him or not. "We're going to set her free," I told him, knowing he'd understand.

It was silent after that. Only my steady breathing could be heard.

We drove for probably twenty minutes in silence before we pulled up in the hospital. Zach parked the vehicle as close to the building as he could before we got out and headed for the door. The building is white with a tan trim lining the outer edge. The parking lot is surprisingly not full. Only a few cars scattered the lot as we walked through the revolving doors.

The first thing I saw was a big tree with birds painted above the large leaves that covered the wall. It then hit me. This is a children's hospital.

After admiring the beautiful art work, I and Zach headed for the front desk where a lady with short curly brown hair sat, typing away on a computer.

"Hello," I greeted the woman who looked to be in her late fifties.

"Hello, dear. How may I help you?" she asked in a thick British accent.

I had almost forgotten that I was actually in London and no longer in Thaxton, Mississippi anymore

"Um, yes. I'm looking for Lily Styles's room," I said, looking into her big brown eyes which were covered by a pair of cat eye glasses.

"Lily Styles?" She repeated my words.

"Yes, Lily Styles. Is there something wrong?" I wondered, raising a brow.

"Oh, no. It's just no one has visited her in almost nine years. We figured her brother must have died for he used to come and see her almost every day," she told me, pushing her glasses further up her nose.

"Oh. Well, who is paying her bills?" I asked, seeking for the answer.

"Her brother put down enough money for her to be put on life support for ten years. We thought it was crazy wasting all that money when the doctors clearly told him there was no hope for her. If she didn't wake up within a month then she never would," she replied.

"But isn't ten years almost up?" I asked, already knowing the answer.

"In a few months, yes."

I knew exactly what would happen once her time was up. They wouldn't let her go on.

"But anyway, you didn't hear all that from me, alright?" The lady whose name tag reads Martha warned.

"Of course," I replied.

"And her room number is 312," she said, pointing towards the elevators. With that, we headed for the lift to take us to the third level where Lily's body lies wasting away.

Once in the elevator, Zach pushed button 3. We both leaned against the back wall of the lift, relaxing to the soft music that plays in the background. Seconds later, we come to a stop. Then the two silver doors parted, letting us out of the small space.

We turned a corner going down a quite long hallway. The door numbers read 309, 310, 311, and before I knew it I was standing in front of 312. Steps away from Lily. Minutes away from her death and seconds away from seeing her for the first time in her human body.

I looked at Zach nodding at me before I grasped the door knob slowly, opening the heavy hospital door. It made a creaky noise against the silent hall.

Once both of us were in the room and standing before her bed, my mouth wanted to hit the floor on seeing what lies in front of me. A young girl, well I should say lady with brown curls cascading down the front of her sheets, lay peacefully in her bed. She had soft features and a small frame. I almost wanted to walk out and say we had the wrong room, but once my eyes caught the end of the bed where a chart was hanging, I knew for a fact that we're in the right room.

The chart contained the following information:

Name: Lily Styles

Date of birth: August 12 ,1997

Admitted to Saint Merry's Children's Hospital: May 7, 2004

Injuries: Third degree burns on face, arms, legs and chest

"Please tell me I'm not the only one who thinks she looks a hell lot like you?" Zach's voice admitted, sounding worried and shocked. I looked at Lily again, knowing good and well that indeed she does look an awful lot like me. "You're not. I see it too."

"Cassandra."

My breathing completely stopped and my heart started to pound as the all too familiar raspy voice that I wish to have never met spoke. Chills run down my spine as I slowly turned around to face the awful man. I looked at him right in the eyes.

"Hunter," I bit back.

"Oh, not happy to see me, are you?" he asked with a smirk I wished to slap off.

"Not at all," I replied, taking a step back.

Zach looked pissed, probably remembering the hits he took from him not long ago.

"Little sassy, aren't we? Been hanging around Zachie a bit too much?" he teased, making Zach clench his fists shut.

"I'll break your pretty face if you don't shut the hell up," Zach threatened in gritted teeth.

"Whatever you say, pretty boy." Hunter smirked, laughing to himself.

I could hear Zach's heavy breathing from across the room. I knew if I don't do something soon someone was going to get hurt.

"What are you doing here?" I asked the first thing that comes to mind.

Hunter took his attention off from a fuming Zach and turned to me. "Coming to see my sister. What are you doing?" he asked, taking a few steps closer which made me want to back up against the wall; but I held back from doing so.

"Setting her free," I replied now having to look up at him from the height difference.

"I don't think so, baby girl." His lips turned into a crooked smile.

"And why not? She's begging to die, she doesn't want to be here anymore, Hunter," I told him, glancing over at her.

"Don't say that," he said, looking at her with teary eyes.

"It's true—"

"Don't!" he yelled, making the room fall silent.

"She's all I have left... She's not allowed to die, I forbid it," Hunter told us, standing before her and brushing her long, curl brown hair.

"Life doesn't work like that, Hunter... It's time to let her go," I slowly started to pull his hands away from her. "Set her free," I whisper in his ear.

I waved to Zach, telling him to find a plug of one of the machines and unplug it. I didn't know if it would work but I was hoping it would. I slowly backed away when the loud beeping could be heard. Her heartbeat was slowing down fast till it was a flat line.

"I'm sorry, Lily," I said as I see her body take one last breath of air before her chest fell still.

"What have you done?" Hunter yelled, shaking his baby sister trying to wake her up; but it's too late.

"It had to be done—"

"You killed her!" He cried, turning to me with tears streaming down his red face.

"You killed my sister!" he shouted, running towards me and shoving me against the hospital wall, his face now only inches from mine. "You killed her." He breathed in my face.

I closed my eyes and said, "She was already dead."

When I reopened my eyes I see Zach pulling Hunter away from me and towards the window, pinning him to it. "Run, Cassandra!" Zach yelled as he had Hunter in a head lock. "Pull the car around back, I'll meet you there," he shouted over Hunter's grunting and cursing.

I turned to run out the door but I was stopped by a voice. "Don't listen to him, Cassie. He's crazier than I am."

When I turned to look at him, his eyes pleaded for me to believe him but my gut told me not to. "I don't think that's humanly possible." With that, I run out of the door hoping not to run into a doctor who had heard the beeping machine. I took the stairs, running down as fast as I possibly could then run out of the lobby without looking back, knowing deep inside me that I was doing the right thing.

Chapter 35

I was just now getting to the parking lot looking in all directions for a black SUV. It seemed that a lot of people had come to the hospital for all the spaces were almost taken.

After spotting the car, I run to it, getting into the driver's seat. I grabbed the keys from under the seat where Zach had left them. Once they were in my hand, I started the car and backed out with ease. I drove around to the back where Zach had told me to go. All I could think about was Zach. Was Zach alright? Had Hunter beaten Zach up again?

I jumped in my seat when a loud knocking started to sound on my window. I looked up half-expecting it to be Hunter but thank God it's Zach. I opened my door.

"Are you alright?" I asked after seeing the cuts on his face.

"I'm fine. Now get in the passenger's seat."

He did just that, buckling his seatbelt right after.

"Where are we going?"

"Don't worry about that, we just need to get away from here."

"Okay," I simply said.

I got comfortable in my seat, trying to rid my mind of the events that just happened. I closed my eyes, not meaning to fall asleep but somehow I did.

***

My eyes shot open to the sound of my mother's voice.

"Cassandra." Her sweet voice spoke my name.

I looked up to see her wearing a long white dress. "Mom?" I asked, knowing it was her just not believing it.

"Yes, dear. It's me," she said, smiling at me.

I got up and ran to her to give her a hug, but when my arms touched her they went straight through. I grimaced at what happened.

"Mom, what's wrong? Why can't I touch you?" I asked on the verge of tears. All I wanted to do was hold her in my arms. It's been so long, I just need a mom hug.

"Oh, my sweet baby girl. Don't you see? We're all waiting for you," she happily told me.

"What do you mean?" I asked, confused, looking around the white room.

"I, your father, and Ben. We're waiting for you, baby." she spoke, her body slowly fading away.

"No wait! Where are you going?" I yelled, a tear streaming down my face.

The room around me started to turn dark. No. Actually, black. The floor beneath me gave up, sending me freefalling into darkness. I closed my eyes, screaming that my lungs ache, waiting for this fall to end then smash onto the ground and die due to the impact; but somehow it never came.

I opened my eyes, looking down only to still see myself falling. How is this possible?

"It isn't," a voice said.

I looked to my right and saw none other than Hunter falling as well.

"H-how did you get here?"

He smirked and said, "I didn't, Cassandra. You're only dreaming."

I looked at him like he's crazy and said, "What?"

"You better wake up or you will be here for real."

And that's when I felt it.

***

The cool water hit my skin, sending chills down my spine. I opened my eyes only to see water quietly rising up inside the car. I went into panic mode and started screaming for help even though I knew no one will hear or see me. I then remembered Zach and looked over to the driver's side only to see him face down in the water.

"Zach!" I yelled, trying to wake him up.

I tried to unbuckle my seatbelt but it's stuck. No. This can't be happening. And that's when the water reached my nose, sending me underwater.

Zach Madden

I looked over to Cassandra to see her peacefully sleeping with her head resting on the window and legs curled up in the seat. She looked so sweet and innocent. I still couldn't believe that bastard Hunter thinks he can just have whoever he wants.

He doesn't know who I am. I'm not just the pretty boy or the stylist. I'm Zach Madden, the man who runs from the police because he kills who he doesn't like. Yes, it's sad and kinda stupid that I kill the people who get on my nerves, but hey, they should learn to be a better person.

Someone who really gets on my nerves is Hunter Stiles. He's the worst of them all. His looks, charm, and him being a lady's man makes me sick. He walks around like he owns the place and talks like he'll actually hurt you, and everybody thinks he will just because he killed his father. People fear him now and it makes me so mad to know that he has everybody wrapped around his finger and that's why I'm going to ruin him.

No, I'm not going to kill him because that would just be too easy. I want him to suffer in a way he had before. I want to kill the only thing he has left, even if it means killing myself as well. The police are after me anyway, I'll be caught soon and thrown into jail.

That's when I saw the bridge.

A smile placed itself in my lips as I looked at Cassandra peacefully sleeping not knowing what was about to happen.

Hunter Stiles

Zach had my girl, the only thing I had left; and I couldn't let him take her from me.

I finally caught up with Zach after driving about fifty, over the speed limit but I didn't care. I focused back on the road when I saw his car. I started to speed up and now we're on a bridge, both driving well over ninety.

My heart stopped when I watched his car swerve over onto the ledge.

Then it happened. His car crossed the guards, sending them flying into the water. I slammed my breaks and jumped out of the car, running to the edge, only to see the car slowly start sinking into the water. I did the first thing that came to mind and jump.

All I could thinking was I must save her. She's all I had left.

Chapter 36

My body landed in the cold water.

I hurried to reach Cassandra who was trapped inside the sinking car. I swam as fast as my body would let me till I' was right in front of the sinking vehicle. I tried opening the door but of course it didn't work from the water pressure.

I cursed under my breath.

I thought quickly and pulled myself on top of the car to see that the sunroof was opened. I slowly lowered myself down into the front seat where Zach sat with head first in the water. I looked to the passenger's side only to see Cassandra doing the same.

I hurried and unbuckled her, failing at my first try but a few more pulls and it released. I lifted her up in my arms then put her over my shoulder and swam back out of the car.

Once back in the ice cold river, I started to swim over to the bank which was close to fifty feet away. I pushed my body faster and harder to swim across the freezing cold water, but it was hard to move plus carrying another person on my back didn't make it any easier.

I could feel Cassie starting to shake and I was glad because that meant she's still alive. I don't know what I would do without her.

I know I've done such cruel and horrible things to her and her family, but I couldn't stop the thoughts that fill my mind. The ones this body have become so fond of. Well, it is basically mine. My body is but my mind isn't. But I'm not doing any of his ideas. I don't like it. I don't like what he tells me to do.

I'm constantly battling "him," the other me. After I hurt her, I scream at myself because I have hurt her again and that's not what I want to do, not at all but she just can't understand that. When I'm hurting her it's not me that's doing it, it's him.

I was now close enough to the bank where I could stand and walk the rest of the way out. I started jogging through the water, my blood pumping fast through my veins, till I was standing on the bank. I run up the big hill which leads to the bridge.

Trees and small bushes blocked my way but I just pushed through them, making cuts appear on my pale skin. Once on the road, I run for the car, still carrying Cassie. I was almost half way there when I heard the sirens go off in a distance. I stopped at the sound of gun shots, thanking that the policeman had a bad aim.

"Put the girl down and raise your hands above your head, Hunter Stiles," the policeman shouted, aiming the gun right at me.

I backed up. "No! She's all I have left," I yelled at them.

Three more police cars pulled up, surrounding the area.

"I can't let you have her," I told them, holding her close to my body.

"If you don't let us take her to a hospital, neither one of us will have her," He told me, seeing the blood dripping from her head.

I followed the stream of blood with my hand, and it leads to her forehead. I kissed the top of her head, holding her close to me.

"Give Cassandra back to us, she needs to see a doctor," One of the police men shouted, slowly walking towards us holding out his hands.

"Come on, Hunter. It's all over, give her to us."

I backed away more. I just couldn't let them have her! "I need her, she's all I have!" I yelled, holding her even closer. Tears started to build behind my eyes and threatening to fall.

"Hunter, she's going to die!" he yelled. "Stop running from your problems and be a man."

"I am a man! I'm trying to protect her," I spoke.

"From who? Who are you trying to protect her from, Hunter?" the officer with jet black hair asked, coming closer.

"From him," I said, pointing to myself. I know they were probably thinking that I'm crazy, and I'm wondering that as well.

"He's crazy," the blonde-headed officer said, shaking his head.

"Maybe I am." I grinned at them. "But I know she can change me. I've felt it before when I'm around her, and we're just talking about life. I feel sane and normal. She can save me." I tried explaining to them while holding her tightly. "And that's why you can't take her from me."

With that, I turned around and run. I run for my life and I run for Cassandra's. I didn't know where I was going but I run. My blood was pumping and my heart felt like it would beat out of my chest but I didn't care. I run till I heard a gunshot, then seconds later it hit me.

I dropped to the ground, Cassandra still held tightly in my arms. My right leg felt like it's on fire. I tried to get up and run away but I couldn't even move my right leg without the sharp pain shooting through it. I looked at Cassandra to see her body shaking and her lips trembling.

I put my left hand on her cheek, slowly inching closer to her, then ever so lightly I pressed my lips to her full, plump pink ones. My lips tingled and my stomach turned in happiness. The feeling truly was hard to describe but was ever so amazing.

Just as the wonderful feeling came, it soon went away. My body was forcefully jerked off to the ground away from Cassandra, and I was thrown into the cop car, my face colliding with the driver's window. I let out a grunt then turned back to where Cassandra was laid only to see an ambulance carrying her away.

"Cassandra!" I cried.

My heart ached at the scene playing in front of me. Needles were being put into her arms and cords all over her body. So much shouting and yelling was going on.

My world started to spin and then it end all at once.

Chapter 37

"Hunter, stop! You're going to make me drop the turkey!" Cassandra scolded, twisting her body around so my arms wre no longer wrapped around her small yet noticeable baby bump.

I let her waist go as she walked to the counter and sat the pan with the turkey down. "Oh come on, it's Christmas!" I said, giving her my famous smirk.

"Stop that." She told me, scrunching up her eyebrows.

"Stop what?" I asked, playing dumb, still holding the smile.

"You know what," she said with a hint of sass.

"You don't like my smile?" I questioned, walking towards her. I wrapped my arms yet again around her stomach.

"Yes, I like your smile but no, I do not like that smirk." She told turning around and tracing my lips.

"You're so sexy." I rasped in her ear biting on it lightly.

"Maybe we should forget the turkey and go upstairs and have a bit a fun, yeah?" I asked, leaving small kisses up and down her neck.

"Hunter, it's Christmas. Stop being so horny," she told me, walking away and over to the fridge.

I watched as her bum bounced perfectly in her yoga pants I had gotten her as an early Christmas gift. I knew they would look sexy as ever on her.

"Just real quick," I pleaded.

She quickly turned around and yelled lightly at me. "No! Hunter, my parents will be here in less than an hour."

I looked down at the ground, hoping to make her feel bad and give in. "What about a kiss?" I asked with puppy dog eyes.

She exhaled quickly before answering. "Yes, you can have a kiss."

I jumped with excitement and hurried over to her, grabbing her waist and ducking her down then slowly kissing her plump pink lips. I deepened the kiss, asking for entrance when—

"Mommy, Daddy! What are you doing?" Sophia, our three-and-a-half-year-old daughter, asked, walking into the kitchen carrying her teddy bear Teddy.

Ben thought she would need it more than him so he let her have it. I thought it was sweet of him after all I did to that child. I'm surprised he even talks to me.

"Loving on each other," I replied to my daughter's question.

"Well, can I be loved on?" she asked, smiling up at the two of us.

"Of course, sweetie." Cassandra said, bending down and picking her up. Even though the doctor said no lifting, Cassie was still determined to hold her first child.

"Give big kisses to Mommy," I said to Sophia and she did just that. We held each other in our arms for as long as possible. Life truly is perfect.

"Stiles, it's time to get up. Now!" I heard a stern voice speak.

I slowly opened my eyes to be met with not a big comfy house with the smell of turkey cooking in the stove and the warmth of family nearby but only the cool dark walls and a hard bed I lay on.

"Get up, your trial is today." It took a minute before everything slowly started to come back to me.

The wreck. Cassandra, Zach getting shot. Going to jail. It all hit at once. "No!" I yelled. *This can't be*, I think to myself.

"Now or else," he spoke sternly to me.

I slowly stood from the bed, walking over to the door. He unlocked it for me then cuffed my hands behind my back.

***

I sat in the courtroom awaiting my fate. I knew what life had in store for me. Next would be bad because they knew about my father and of course they knew I kidnaped Cassandra and Ben. I just didn't think I could live my life in jail. I would go insane if I do.

I heard my name being called so I made my way to the stand. I sat before the judge and the jury who stare blankly at me.

As I was looking at the people sitting before me, I spotted two familiar faces. It's Cassandra's parents. Her mother was holding back tears, and her father just glared at me. I looked away from the hard stares.

"Well, well, Mr. Hunter Lee Stiles. We've been looking for you for years, you know that right?" the judge asked.

"Yes, sir." I replied. I knew bad manners wouldn't help my case so I was polite.

"It seems you've gotten yourself in even more trouble than the last time I heard your name. You've kidnapped, beaten, and sexually—"

"I did not sexually assault her," I interrupted. I heard a sniffle come from the small crowd, it being her mother.

"Let me finish, Stiles," he spoke glaring at me.

"Yes, Sir." I sat back in my chair, knowing I just needed to let this blow over.

"You've kidnapped, beaten, and sexually assaulted a young girl by the name of Cassandra Lowe. Is this true?" he asked, pushing his glasses to the end of his fat nose.

"No, sir," I answered truthfully.

"Really?" he asked, acting surprised that would be my answer.

"I never touched her, your honour."

He flipped through papers, reading, before speaking. "At the age of fourteen you were diagnosed to be psychotic. After killing your father you were then sent to a mental institution for two years until you escaped, then you were never seen again until just a few days ago. Now is that true?"

"Yes, sir. It is." I admitted.

"Now it says here you are still messed up in the head, and when you killed your father you didn't truly know what you were doing. You said to the nurse that a demon was telling you to do it." He chuckled to himself. "I don't think being psycho is an actual thing. I just thought some people like to use their dark imagination a bit more than others, but it says here you do have mental issues and that you were not in control of your body."

I know the paper is right, I wasn't. It was him. He did it, he made me do the horrible things.

"So with that said, Hunter, for the kidnaping and beating of Cassandra Lowe and the murder of Devon Stiles, seven years with psychosis mental brain damage." He hit the gavel on its wooden stand two times then stood to leave the courtroom, filled with yelling and cussing towards the judge, but I was thankful.

Only seven years, I guess that disorder does have its ups. I'd be out before I know it.

Chapter 38

Sometimes life isn't fair with the things thrown at us. Friends lie, people die, lovers cheat, and yet the world doesn't stop turning. Now, if the world would stop and ask us, how is your life? Or can I change something for you? And everything is just given to us the way we want it, I believe the world would be very boring and bland. We would all be spoiled with the things we always wished to have, and that's why I sometimes don't mind not always getting what I want because I've learned that everything good comes in time.

So as I lay in my cell, waiting for seven years to pass so I could finally go out and find my love again, I would just have to wait and think of all the sweet things I would tell her. I'd planned out every word down to the last of how I will sweep her off her own two feet, my words laced with love and care towards her.

Oh, what a wonderful day that would be. I could see it now, my past behind me. No more killing or harming young girls, only love and affection towards them will be shown, and only seven years till that day.

Cassandra's Mother

I sat impatiently as I stared at her from my sitting position in the chair across her hospital bed, waiting for my daughter to open her big eyes.

When I heard the news about her and Ben being kidnapped, I dropped what I was doing and fell to my knees crying. At that moment I thought I had lost my two children.

Thankfully, the police had found their taker and now he's sitting in prison for seven years. He should have to stay longer. Seven years isn't really that long compared to some who get thirty, but now I can only wait.

The doctor said that she should wake up in a few days from this coma she seemed to fall in. He said it was from shock and possibly from the wreck. I could only pray that she'd wake up from this, I don't think I could go on as a mother knowing I outlived one of my children.

I'm thankful that Ben is alright. I know his life would never be the same from the loss of his right leg, but he'll be alright. He'll need a lot of help till he gets used to his new prosthetic leg, but he'll live; and that's all that matters to me.

Chapter 39

Cassandra

I've never really been afraid of much. Yes, when I was little, the dark scared me and so did clowns, but when it came to pain or dying it never really bothered me till today when my mind woke up but my body didn't. I could hear, think, and dream but I couldn't move, talk, or see. It's scary really, being able to hear your mother's prayers and your father's disbelief as he talked to himself.

The doctors would come in for a few moments to check up on me but never realized I was mentally awake. I'd been working on moving my feet, hoping that if I start from the bottom and work my way up maybe I could wake my stiff body up. As I was sitting there trying to move my toes, something wonderful happened. They move. I could feel them and before I knew it I was starting to move my legs, then chest, and all of a sudden my eyes opened. The bright light from the large glass window blinded me but I didn't care. I'd been sitting here in darkness for too long.

I heard my mother gasp and then she run over to my side, bending down and embracing me. I hugged her back as tight as I could. She was whispering I love you over and over in my ear. Soon after, my father joined hugging me tight as well.

"Oh, my baby. I've been so worried. You have no idea how much I missed you and your brother." She cried in my shoulder.

"Ben? What happened to him?" I asked, clueless as to what was wrong with my little brother.

My mother and father pulled away from me, looking strangely at me like I had said something stupid.

"You don't remember?" they asked at the same time.

Just then the doctor walked in. A surprised expression was written on his features when he saw that I was awake.

"Well, look who's woke up," he cheered, making his way over to my bed.

"There's something wrong," my mother quickly said, standing from her sitting position.

"Alright, and what is it? Because she looks fine to me," he told her, smiling over at me making the wrinkles around his mouth and eyes show.

"She can't remember what happened," my mother said, panic written on her soft features.

"Well it looks like it's only short term memory for she remembers you all and that's good. It's probably better that she doesn't know what happened, she'll get through this faster with the less she knows," he told both my stressing parents.

"Well, what does she remember? Anything?" my father spoke.

"We'll just have to ask her and see." The doctor smiled at me.

"Alright, Cassandra. What were you doing on December 1?" John, my doctor, asked me.

I thought back to that day then answered as best as I could.

"Well, I had just got out of school. My mom and dad were leaving for Australia that night and I remember being mad at her because she had hired a sitter when clearly I didn't need one. When I got home, I ate then sat around waiting for the sitter and that's all I remember. I and Ben were just watching TV and after that it's all blank."

"I see. Well, the good news is you're fine and the bad news is you did lose some of your memory but really, that's better."

I couldn't believe I had forgotten some of my life when it had just happened like a month ago. How could this be?

Later that night, I didn't sleep well thinking about all the things I had forgotten. It scared me, not knowing. It really did. I could only hope it comes back because I really would like to know what happened a month ago.

Chapter 40

Locked away in a prison cell was a young man, sitting, counting the days till he would be free from the bars that hold him back from his love. With only a pen and a pad of paper, he wrote. To her, the girl who holds his heart.

But she was unaware of the precious and broken heart she holds as she opened the door to a home she could barely call her own. A young boy came rolling to her side, sitting in his wheelchair with only one leg and a prosthetic one. They held each other tight. She tried letting go only to be held tighter. Little did she know what her and her brother had gone through?

They were finally back to being a family, a happy one at that, with only a lost leg, some added bruises and scars that may never fade, and a few memories that will never appear; but they were a family brought back together by law and broken by a man that was claimed to be psycho, but really was just never understood.

So seven years he waited, and seven years she moved on, forgot, and more importantly lived. She lived without a silly and naive love for a man who could never treat her right or be loved the way she deserves. So she waits as well, but for a love worth telling. Not one that would be tragically plastered on every newspaper and news channel on how the young and naive girl fell for a man who was psychotically crazy in the head.

Six Years Later

Cassandra

I found myself slowly zoning out as Leah, a fifteen year old girl, told her life story. She poured her heart out to me, pointing out every mark on her body, telling me what each one was for and who gave them to her. I couldn't help but envy her, the way she knows where the scars came from and who had marked her body.

I so wished I knew who gave me mine. This scar on my forehead or the one on my hip, but no, nothing. I couldn't remember anything and even worse, my family stayed quiet and would just say the cat did it but I know they're lying.

Something bad, no, horrible, happened in my life. They were keeping it from me and it made me want to go crazy some days. The fear of not knowing who did this or why ate me alive. Is this person still out there waiting to get me? Will my memory come back one day while I'm just walking home alone itself and scare me? Why can't I remember? Why?

Everything else in my life was going great. I got the apartment I wanted, and the job.

Being a therapist for troubled teens is an amazing job but it also makes me wonder even more. They tell me their stories; and I couldn't help but wonder if mine is similar, maybe my father beat me and I just lost my memory. What if I took some kind of pill that made me higher than Mount Everest and I just happened to have some loss of memory?

"Cassandra, are you listening?" Leah's voice broke my train of thought.

I snapped out of my daze and looked at her. "What? Oh, yes."

A questioning look played on her soft features.

"I'm sorry I keep zoning out, I just have a lot on my mind," I said truthfully.

"I understand, there're some days where I can't even think straight."

I smiled at her and said, "Well, I'm having one of those days."

"I can tell." She laughed lightly. "Well, what's on your mind?" she asked, crossing her arms over her chest, mocking me.

"I think that it's my job to ask you that," I said.

"Well it seems the tables have turned." She smiled then put her serious face back on. "Now, tell me."

I thought hard on whether I should tell this young girl my problems or not. Would it really hurt? It's not like I knew enough for it to even matter. "Well, it seems I have forgotten a short time of my life from when I was your age. I woke up in a hospital, not being able to remember the past month but was left with scars from unknown things; and still to this very day, six years later, I wonder who did this to me," I admitted truthfully to the young girl.

"I see... I know why you're afraid, I would be too; but I think you're a very strong woman, Cassandra, and one day you'll figure this out but for now I guess it's just another mystery waiting to be solved."

I took in her words, letting them sink in. Maybe she was right, maybe this is just a mystery that's waiting to be solved; or perhaps I won't ever know what happened and maybe, just maybe, that's for the better. "Thank you, Leah." I stood and embraced her.

"You're very welcome." Just as she said that my phone beeped notifying that her time was up.

We said our goodbyes before I sat back down and thought on what she told me and told myself it's just a mystery. One day I'll figure it out.

The door opened, my next patient was here to see me and tell me about their problems. I'd write them down on a piece of paper and help them get through whatever horrible thing brought them here.

My heart breaks for some young girls who only wanted to be loved but sadly were given the responsibility of taking care of a child at such a young age, that not even I would be ready for. Or the boys who are beaten by their own father, a result of the drunken state—

"Hello, Cassie." An all too familiar raspy voice interrupted my thoughts.

I looked up to be met with curly hair and piercing green eyes staring back at me.

"It's been a while, Cass." The oddly familiar-looking man smirked at me from across the small room.

The only thing going through my mind was this is the man who scarred my body and was taken from my memory. This is Hunter Stiles.

Chapter 41

As I stood before the man I believe had scarred my body, I started to think, what if it isn't? Maybe he just looked familiar. His hair was in loose curls swooped over to one side, he's wearing jet black pants with a white top that says "Rolling Stones" on the front, his arms were covered in tattoos, and he had one lip ring. His now soft, green eyes met mine before his heart-shaped lips form words.

"I guess I should probably introduce myself. I'm Lee."

When the name left his lips I could finally let out the breath I didn't know I was holding in. So it wasn't him, only a look alike.

"Well it seems you know my name already." I chuckled lightly.

"Cassandra, am I right?"

I nodded my head yes, still feeling a bit uneasy about his presence.

"So tell me, Lee, how do I know you? I've had a bit of memory loss," I admitted. I looked down, a bit embarrassed.

"We met at a party back in the beginning of 2014," he said.

I thought back to it and couldn't remember ever going to a party, let alone talking to such a nice looking man.

"I'm sorry but it must be my touch of amnesia, there's a part in my life back in 2014 when I lost a bit of memory. That might be why I don't know you."

"Oh, well. That's alright," he said awkwardly, looking around the room.

I started to bite on my bottom lip, wondering if I should say anything else or just let him speak next. For some reason this man made me feel nervous and very uncomfortable from his good looks and deep stare.

"Would you, maybe, want to get some coffee?" his raspy voice asked, still staring deep into my soul.

I debated on what to say, should I just agree and go with him? Or make up an excuse to get away from this awkwardness? I deiced to go with the second and just use an excuse.

"I have to work, I'm sorry," I said. It was true, I did have to finish, even if I did get off in ten minutes. I still wasn't lying, was I?

"Oh, okay. Well maybe when you get off?"

Shoot, why did he have to ask that? Now what do I do? Think, Cassandra, think.

"Oh, uh, I'm sorry, I have, uh... dinner with my parents! After work." I couldn't believe I thought of that excuse so quickly. Good thinking, Cassandra.

"You aren't just making up excuses, Cassie. Are you?" Lee asked the spot-on question.

Of course I was! I didn't want to get coffee with a complete stranger! I did know what he might do to me. "Why would you think that?" I asked, playing dumb, but I knew he wasn't stupid. He could see right through me.

"If you don't want to go get coffee then you should have just said so. It's no biggy, even though I would like to get to know you better, Cass." The way he said my old nickname made my heart flutter and stomach turn, but in a good way I think?

"I, uh... just coffee, right?" I asked slowly giving in.

"Just coffee."

With that, I grabbed my coat and purse, telling the front desk I was leaving earlier even though it was only five minutes; but Lee didn't need to know that.

We got to the parking lot. There was a storm coming. The sky was dark with black and grey clouds filling it and a light rain coming down. We hurried and ran across the lot, him leading the way to his vehicle. It was an old red truck, a bit banged up and some paint chipped but in drivable shape.

He opened the door for me and shut it then ran around to the other side to open his as well. I put my seatbelt on and tried to get as comfy as possible in the small space. Lee put the key in the ignition, trying to start the old truck.

At first it wouldn't, but not long after a few tries, it finally started. He pulled out of the lot, heading for the main road. I still couldn't believe I agreed to go get coffee with him, let alone get in a car with a complete stranger, but something intrigued me about him.

"What kind of music do you like?" he asked, flipping through the radio stations.

"Sad, meaningful songs," I answered, knowing in no way that he liked them as well.

"Really? Sad songs? Isn't that a bit depressing?" he asked, glancing over at me.

"Not when they mean something to you," I replied.

I love sad songs ever since I got out of the hospital I'd gone to them for help. I heard a song similar to my life and automatically fell in love with it.

"What about rap?" He turned the station to one playing music I could barely understand, let alone think to myself.

"Not really my thing," I admitted truthfully. "To me, it has no meaning."

Lee quickly turned to me with shock written on his features. "What? How so?"

"Like, it just doesn't. For one, you can't even understand half the time what they're saying and two, they're all about sex and drugs." I knew he wouldn't like it but it was the truth.

"Not true," he said as we pulled up to the small brick building with the name "Coffee & Cakes."

We got out and run to the door, trying to stay dry as possible, but it was pretty hard from the rain coming down so hard.

As the door opened, a bell rung. We walked in, looking around. Only an elderly couple sat sipping on hot coffee and cookies.

Lee found a seat by the window. I walked over to the table, taking a seat to where I could still see out.

"Hi, I'm Katie, and welcome to Coffee & Cakes. Can I start you off with hot chocolate? Maybe a latte or a hot cup of coffee?" she asked.

I looked over at Lee to see if he was going to order first but he didn't so I did.

"Um, yes. A caramel latte would be great," I said.

"Alrighty, and for you, sir?" she asked him, twirling her long blonde hair between her fingers. She liked him, I could tell. I mean, why wouldn't she? He's very nice looking and a kind man.

"Yeah, I'll just have a hot chocolate," he said, handing her our menus.

"Okay, I'll have these out in no time!" She winked at him then quickly ran off to the back of the restaurant.

"Well that was a bit awkward," I stated, looking out the window to see the storm lighting up a bit.

"Ha ha, you're telling me." He chuckled lightly.

It was silent for a minute, neither one of us daring to speak a word; but when he did, it shocked me to hear what came out of his mouth.

"You're a beautiful girl, Cassandra."

Chapter 42

When the five simple words left his mouth, I was so shocked I probably turned red as a tomato. I didn't really know what to say, so I replied with a thank you.

He looked at me with a smirk etched on his features. "You're very welcome, Cassie."

It just then hit me that he was calling me by my nickname, something I hadn't been called in years. So I asked, "Who told you my nickname?"

Something flashed across his eyes. Maybe shock? Or was it fear? But whatever it was disappeared fast before he answered, "At the party, you insisted I call you it." The party. Something I still could not recall ever going to.

"Who was having the party again?" I pushed further, wanting so badly to know.

"Summer was," He replied.

I thought back to my best friend, wondering how he knew her. I was tempted to ask but decided that I'd better not. Oh was all I said.

Minutes later, our drinks had come and we were sipping on them till they were completely empty. Lee got up and paid the flirtatious blonde who I saw wrote her number on the receipt, handing it to him. I got up from my chair, heading for the door, Lee opening it for us.

The rain had stopped, and a rainbow had appeared, making the harsh weather worth the beauty of the colorful view.

"Well, thank you for the latte. I can pay you if you want?" I offered.

"No, no. It's on me," He insisted.

We walked back to his old truck, getting in. I made sure to buckle up.

"So you really don't remember me?" he asked, looking over at me from the driver's side.

I thought about it for a moment knowing in fact, I did not know this man. I think I would be able to recall such a nice looking face.

"No, I'm very sorry." The touch of amnesia had really been starting to bug me since Lee showed up.

"Well then, I would love to start over. Will you start over with me too?"

A spark of hope flashed in his green iris. "That would be nice."

I smiled his way to only see his pearly whites on full show.

"You have nice teeth." It wasn't supposed to come out, but it did anyway.

"Well, thank you. You have a very nice smile, something I would love to see more often," he complimented.

I just blushed and whispered, "thank you" before turning my attention towards the window, gazing up at the beautiful rainbow that had planted itself in the sky. It was quiet the rest of the way back to my work, I wasn't complaining though. I liked peace and quiet more than talking as long as there was music to listen to, which there was. I'm perfectly fine with silence.

I got out of his beaten-up truck, saying one last thank you before heading towards my old midnight blue Honda. But before I could even reach the handle, I was stopped by a voice.

"Hey, wait up," Lee's voice called out to me.

I turned around to see him jogging to my car. Once he was standing in front of me, he breathed out. "I was just wondering what your number is because I know, to you, we just met but to me it's different. You may not remember, but we talked a lot and you told me a lot about yourself. So please," he asked, holding out his phone.

He was biting hard on his bottom lip, and I wanted him to stop before it drew blood so I answered quickly for the sake of his plump, heart-shaped lips.

"Ah... yeah, sure." I smiled at him.

We exchanged numbers and said our goodbyes before both of us got into our old outdated cars.

I buckled up and started out of the parking lot, heading to my apartment.

* * *

I opened the door, throwing my keys on a side table beside the entrance before going to my room and plopping down, face first, on my bed. I lay there, thinking back on everything that happened today with Lee.

Nothing really made sense. I know it's just from my memory loss, but it really got to me that I couldn't remember him. He seemed like such a sweet guy; but then again, I don't know him.

I had no idea what kind of guy he really is. For all I know, he could be a murderer but he also could be the sweetest guy to ever walk this earth. Well, that may be a little bit much but still.

Just then, I heard my phone ding, notifying me that I got a text, the name reading, "(***) *** **** unknown."

I opened the text, it reading, "Guess who? xx"

I knew then exactly who it was because I had only given out my number once and that was to Lee, but I decided to play around a bit by saying, "Is it Santa Claus?"

I sent the message, lying flat on my back now. Seconds later, my phone dinged again. This time text message reading, "If you want then yes. xx"

I didn't really understand the "xx" but went with it anyway. "I think I like Lee better ;)"

Not even two minutes after sending, it I had a reply. "How do you know my name?! xx"

I could tell he was messing with me so I went along with it. "How'd you get my number?"

He replied, "How about dinner tomorrow night my place? xx"

Once I read the message, I read it over and over not believing that he would ask that right out of the blue.

"Random much?" I sent it, wondering why a man, like Lee, would want me over at his house.

"Maybe a little but no, what's your answer, ma'am? Xx"

I thought about it, did I really want to go to a stranger's house? No, not a stranger's house but yes to Lee's. Was this a bad idea? Probably. But what's holding me back? Nothing. So I replied with, "sure sounds great! What time?"

And he answered with, "seven see ya then xx"

So I was now having dinner with a total complete stranger who happened to be smoking hot. Wonderful.

Chapter 43

It was currently 6:15 pm, and I was just now starting to get ready.

My hair was wrapped up tightly in a blue towel while it air dries a bit. I decided to start my makeup, just barely applying foundation under my eyes then moving on to my brows. I'd always had full brows so I just brushed the big bushes out and moved on to the eyeshadow.

I did a smoky eye and applied a thick black line above my lashes and on my waterline. After one coat of mascara, I was done and moving on to my hair. I blew dried it, my natural curls falling loosely right above my breasts. I put some oil on my hair to make it shine. It seemed to do the trick. Now I just needed to find something to wear.

I walked over to my small closet, which was in need of a light because you can't see anything in here. I ripped out dresses and lace tops, everything seeming not good enough for this little date I was going on in less than ten minutes. My royal blue dress stood out from the rest so I picked it up, taking it off the hanger and slipping the silk-like material on. It hugged my curves then flared out at the bottom which ends a couple of inches above the knee. I took out a pair of black flats, since me and heels do not mix.

There's a knock on the door, and I knew exactly who it was. I walked to the entrance, taking my time so I don't seem too eager. I opened the door to find Lee standing there in all black with the front of his shirt unbuttoned down to the middle of his stomach, where tattoos are visible.

"Well, don't you look stunning!" he complimented me, my cheeks turning red.

"You too," I said back.

"You ready for a night with Stiles?" That sounded wrong.

But I just brushed it off saying, "styles?" I was confused.

"Yes, Stiles. My last name is Stiles," he filled me in.

So, Lee Stiles. I felt like something was just missing there, but I pushed the thought aside and grabbed my coat, locking the door behind me.

Lee opened the passenger door for me and I slipped in his old truck, buckling my seat belt. He did the same and started the vehicle, and it roared to life.

"So, where to?" I asked, glancing over at him.

"It's a surprise," he answered.

I didn't try and get the answer out of him, knowing we'd be there soon enough.

Ten minutes later, we pulled up to a cute little restaurant that is located between two brick buildings, the name reading, "Cobbler Cafe." We got out, walking side by side to the door.

It was incredibly small but very cute. Only a few tables lined the walls, pictures hung on the brick, and the smell coming from the kitchen was amazing. We took a seat by the door, us being the only people in here. A waitress with short brown hair came, walking over with two menus in hand.

"Hello, I'm Missy. Welcome to Cobbler Cafe. Can I start you off with something to drink? Maybe a coke or sweet tea?" the bubbly girl asked, her ray of happiness bringing my mood up a notch.

"I'll have a sweet tea," I answered the young girl.

"And I'll have the same," Lee added.

Missy ran off to the back, leaving me and Lee to scan the menus for something good to eat. Everything looked great, to be honest.

"Would you maybe want to share a large, thin crust pizza? I've had them before and they're fantastic!" He smiled widely at me.

"That sounds great," I agreed to the pizza.

Lee ordered our food when Missy came back with our drinks.

"So tell me about yourself," he asked, staring at me.

I thought for a moment. What would interest him? There's really not much to me since he already knows where I work so I had to think hard on this question.

"Honestly, there's really not much to me," I answered, giving up on what I could tell him.

He looked at me thoughtfully. "There must be something you can tell me."

"There really isn't anything. I'm twenty-three years old, I enjoy my job as a therapist, and I have a younger brother who is fourteen, named Ben." That's all I could think of on the spot. Boring, yes. But at least it's something.

"Well I'm twenty-six, I currently work at this little music store in the mall, and I have no siblings," he told me.

"It must have been boring growing up with no brothers or sisters."

I don't know what I would have done without Ben. I loved taking care of him when he was a baby.

"Actually, I had a younger sister but she died."

I instantly felt bad for asking, that must have been awful.

"Oh, I'm so sorry."

"It's fine, really. It happened a long time ago." He frowned.

It was silent till our food came. Missy happily set the pizza on the small table, and we ate in silence, neither one of us knowing what to say. I regretted ever asking him about siblings.

Lee got up and paid Missy for the food. I walked out to the car, knowing the ride home would probably be awkward as well. He came walking towards the car saying, "Let's go for a walk."

I agreed, following him down the vacant walkway, the night cool breeze piercing through my thin coat. I should have brought something warmer since it was November.

"I'm sorry for making dinner so awkward. Just... When my sister is brought up, it just brings back bad memories." He finally spoke up.

"Cassie, I think you're the most beautiful, smart, and kindhearted girl I've ever known and I just want you to know that."

My heart melted at his sweet words, my cheeks blushing. "Thank you, Lee. And I think you're a very wonderful man that I can't wait to get to know more of." He smiled at me. Not just any smile but a true, genuine smile.

"Thank you, Cass."

We walked hand in hand in the small park with only the moon and the occasional light pole. It was peaceful out here, so quiet.

"I hope you'll go on another date with me," Lee said after the silence.

"Well I believe I get to pick the next place," I said smiling at him.

We stopped on a bench in front of a water fountain, the liquid frozen from the winter air. Lee looked deeply at me, putting one hand on my cheek, caressing it. He leaned in and I panicked. Was he really going to kiss me?

No, he couldn't. I pulled back, standing from my sitting position.

"Well, it's getting late. We better go."

"Oh, okay." We walked back awkwardly.

Why did I have to do that? I bet he kisses amazingly.

We get in his truck, the ride home silent. He walked me up to my apartment and stopped at the door saying, "I... I," he began to speak but couldn't seem to finish what he was going to say.

"Cassandra—Dang it," he cursed at himself before grabbing my face and pushing me against my apartment door.

Chapter 44

I was shocked at first as his warm lips move against mine. His lips played with mine as I stood there, limp from shock. My brain finally kicked in, telling me to kiss the man back. I put my left hand on his chest and my right somehow got tangled in his curly locks. We kissed for a good twenty seconds before we both pulled away. Lee rested his forehead on mine as our breaths collided. His eyes locked with mine before giving me one last quick kiss before leaving without a word. I stood there in utter shock as I was left alone outside my apartment.

Did Lee really just kiss me? Did I really get a kiss by this smoking hot man? The way his lips moved with mine was unlike anything I'd ever felt before. The tingly feeling that his lips left on mine is a feeling I wouldn't mind having all the time.

A gust of wind brought me back to reality. I unlocked my door and headed for my bedroom. I took off my coat, throwing it on my duvet. When it landed, a small folded-up piece of paper fell out of it. I tilted my head at it walking over to my bed, picking the thin white slip of paper up. I unfolded it and read.

"Let's do this again sometime — H." I read it over and over.

"H?" Who's that? Lee must have put in it my pocket because I hadn't been with anyone else today; so instead of going to bed, I grabbed my laptop off of my decks and pull up Google People. I typed in **Lee Stiles**. About two hundred people popped up. I looked through them, none of the men being my Lee.

There's a website that lets you describe the person you're looking for so I clicked on it and filled out the entry boxes. Once done, I read over what I had written. "**Male, brown curly hair, green eyes, height around 6'3**. Name: **Lee Stiles**." I pushed enter, and the website was now loading.

New men with that description popped up, only twenty men showed. I read through them. Some were obviously a no or their age didn't match Lee's. After going through all of them, the website soon changed and sent me to a newspaper article with the headline reading, "Hunter Lee Stiles charged with kidnapping of Cassandra and Ben Lowe."

My mouth dropped as I saw the photo placed below. It's a picture of me and Ben at a gas station with Lee. It's obvious that the picture was from a security camera. I finished reading the article, my head full of all sorts of questions. This couldn't be Lee, it just couldn't be! He was so nice and sweet.

"Oh, God. I let the man who kidnapped me and my brother kiss me." I couldn't believe what I was saying even though I knew it was true.

I pushed on another link which lead me to yet another article about him. "Hunter Stiles sent to prison for six years was released today, November 21." The day he was released was also the day he showed up at my work, he came straight to me.

"Hunter Stiles went into prison as a kidnaper and possible murderer, further crimes are not being said requested by Mr. Stiles himself. The guards at the prison say he came out a changed man, you would never thought he had done all those awful things," the reporter said as I watch a short YouTube video.

"Cassandra's family was contacted earlier today before his release, warning them that he was out. We asked how Cassandra was, wondering how she is doing. They replied with, 'She's doing great. The car accident she was in with Mr. Stiles caused her some memory loss so she doesn't recall a thing about the kidnapping with her and her brother.'"

I couldn't believe all these years I'd been wondering what happened to me and Ben and I finally find out but this way? Really? An article?!

Were my parents ever going to tell me? Is Lee coming after me again? Is that why he's trying to get close to me so he can just kidnap me again? So many questions were spinning in my head, I just did't know where to begin.

I put my laptop away, no longer wanting to see any more about this. I lay down in bed with my clothes still on but at this point I didn't care. All I could think about before I fell asleep was, whatever I do, Don't fall for Hunter Lee Stiles.

* * *

I woke up to the sound of my phone buzzing on my desk beside me. I grabbed it, answering before I even look at the name.

The voice on the other end spoke with a deep rasp, and I knew exactly who it was.

"L-Lee," I stuttered his middle name.

"Cassie! Good morning! I'm so sorry for running off so quick last night," he spoke shyly through the phone.

"Oh, it's alright," I said.

"Well I thought, maybe, we could hang out later?"

I knew I couldn't say yes but how could I say no? "I, uh... Hunt—I mean Lee. I don't think we need to talk anymore." I was screwed. I heard movement on the other end before the slam of a door.

"I'm coming over." And with that he hung up.

I hurried off of my bed, knowing I was in deep shit. I grabbed my baseball bat and my bottle of pepper spray and waited on the couch for him to arrive.

Chapter 45

I sat quietly on the couch alone, playing with my hands still not believing that Lee, I mean Hunter, kidnapped me and Ben. I wished I could remember more of the day he came into my life.

I knew it was the last day of school and I was mad at my mother because I had to watch Ben while they were going to Ghana. I remembered them leaving and my mother asking me if I could handle being alone with Ben. Of course I just rolled my eyes replying with a "yes, mother" but after that I couldn't recall the babysitter ever showing up.

I had been having these dreams, vivid ones about me at some kind of big building with girls in little to no clothes and men shouting as they beat a young girl. When I wake up from these dreams, I'm drenched with sweat and shaking. Last night it was different, though, this time I was in a car with a man. He had dark hair with big brown eyes, he was gorgeous but he seemed almost mad? Crazy? Maybe, I really don't know what was wrong with him but someone was chasing us in a car and that's when the dark-haired man drove us over the bridge, and right when our car hit the water, I woke up to the sound of my phone ringing.

It's silent for a while. I myself was having trouble thinking of anything to worry about, but soon there's a knock on the door, more like a banging.

"Cassie, let me in!" I heard Hunter's voice yell through the hard wood.

I slowly rose from my sitting position on the couch and walked slowly towards the door.

"Cass, I'm not going to hurt you. I promise."

I was almost to the door now. "I don't believe you!" I yelled. Tears started to build up.

"Please, Cassie. Give me a second chance. I won't hurt you, you know that, right?"

My hands were shaking and my breathing was far from normal. "How can I trust you? You've hurt me and my family so much! Why should I trust you?" Tears were on the verge of pouring down in my face even though I hadn't even seen the man that caused them today.

"I know it's hard but you just have to trust me," he pleaded. "Please, Cass."

I sat the baseball bat down and laid the pepper spray on the table beside the door. My hands came in contact with the lock, slowly undoing it until a click could be heard. I turned the knob hesitantly and stepped away from the door, turning my back to him before my eyes came in contact with his. I heard footsteps, then a door shutting. The floor creaked as his weight balanced between boards. A hand placed itself on my shoulder but I flinched away from it softly saying, "Don't touch me." The hand removed itself from me and then the clearing of a throat sounded.

"Cassie—" Hunter spoke, resting his large hand back where I just said to remove it from.

"I said, don't touch me," I spoke, trying to keep cool and hold back the tears which were still trying to pour down my face.

"Cassandra, please listen to me!" he pleaded, turning me around by my shoulders.

I refused to look him in the eyes though.

"Look at me. Please," he spoke softly. I kept my gaze on the hard wood.

"Fine," he breathed out, gently grabbing my face to make me look at him. My hair cascaded over my pale skin as my green eyes locked with his for a mere second before I closed them.

"I know there is nothing I can say or do for you to forgive me—"

"You're right, there isn't. So leave. I don't want you here," I said, barely holding back the tears. I pulled away from his grasp only for him to grab at my waist.

"Stop touching me! Don't you see you're not wanted here?" I yelled, turning to face him. My breathing was heavy and my face was probably red from anger and hurt.

"I—"

"You lied! You hurt me and my family. You took away my brother's leg!" I screamed at him but I didn't care, not one bit. He deserved it.

"Cassandra, listen to me!" He grabbed my shoulders, shaking me. "I'm sorry—"

"No, you're not—" I stopped mid-sentence as his hand raised from his side coming right to my left cheek. My eyes widened and so did his, but right as he was inches away he stopped, and that's when the tears poured.

I broke down, crying as everything slowly started to come back. The way he hit me and Ben and yelled at us for nothing, when he shot at us in the woods and he missed me but hit my brother, when we tried to escape fr60 him by crawling out the back window when the car broke down, and the warehouse where girls were forced to entertain and have sex with men they'd never met before. Everything came back in one big flashback.

"I wasn't going to hit you," he said in panic as he noticed the horrified expression I had plastered on my face.

I just turned away from him, running over to the door, but he grabbed me by the waist, pulling me to him.

"No! Let me go!" I cried, clawing at the air but he just held me tighter.

I struggled to reach for the table after seeing what I needed on it. My fingers stretched and caught the bottle of pepper spray. I turned around and sprayed him right in the eyes. He screamed in pain, covering his face. I run to my room, locking the door behind me. I searched for my car keys, I knew I left them in here. I looked on my bed and on the side table but they were nowhere to be found. I heard banging on the door and cries coming from Hunter. I did feel bad, but what else was I gonna do?

"Cassandra, please. Help me!" he screamed.

I was surprised the neighbors hadn't called the cops yet.

"Cassie, it burns!"

Tears were still falling down my cheeks as I heard his cries on the other side of the door.

"I know I did wrong and I know you will never forgive me but, Cassandra, I changed. You may not believe me, but I did and I know you will never have the feelings I have for you but just know."

He stopped crying for a moment as he paused mid-sentence. "Just know, I love you and always will."

My heart broke into pieces even though it shouldn't have. I crawled into my bed, wrapping myself in blankets as tears still poured. I felt sick but not like throwing up sick, I felt heart broken.

But why? Because I formed some kind of soft spot for Hunter before I knew it was him? Or is it because I just felt bad for making him cry? I really didn't know. I closed my eyes, wishing for sleep to take me away from this world; but right before it did, I heard Hunter faintly say, "He's gone."

Chapter 46

The next morning I woke up to the sun shining on my pale skin.

I stretched my arms out in front of me, yawning, and then slowly got out of bed. I headed to my bathroom which is located on the opposite side of the room. I used the bathroom then brush my teeth. I threw my hair up in a loose bun and headed for the kitchen. When I opened my bedroom door, I let out a scream as Hunter lay sprawled out on my floor. He woke up from the sound of my voice, and everything slowly started to come back from last night.

His words played over and over in my head. "He's gone." Hunter jumped up from the floor and grabbed for the door as I closed it; but I was not fast enough, he already has his foot wedged between the door and my bedroom wall. I screamed for him to stop but he won't.

"Hunter, stop!" I screamed but he didn't listen.

"Just let me in!" he said, pushing harder on the door.

"No! You hurt me, Hunter, and I will never forgive you!" I said with rage evident on my face, but tears were threatening to spill over. I just couldn't do this anymore, I want to have my old life back. The life before any of this happened, before Hunter, before life happened. I just want to be little again. I don't want this life anymore.

Hunter slowly stopped pushing on the door, I stopped too. I could hear his heavy breathing on the other side.

"I can't believe you won't forgive me even though I've changed." He sounded broken and it broke me to hear him like this.

"If you've changed then why did you try to hit me? If you've truly changed, why, Hunter?" I asked, emotion laced with every word I spoke.

"He's gone but... Sometimes he comes back, and I can't control it but I'm better, I promise. I wouldn't be here if knew I was putting you in danger." He sounded genuine about it but it was still difficult to trust him with all that he put me through.

"How can I trust you?" I asked. "How, Hunter?"

It was silent, only the sound of our uneven breaths could be heard. Was I really considering trusting him after all that he put me through? In a way, I wanted to because maybe he has changed, but the other part of me was screaming at me saying for me to run as far as away from him I as can. Something was telling me otherwise.

"I love you." Three simple words he said with passion and brokenness of the heart. "I love you and I know you'll never love me back and that's not okay, but I guess it has to be because I'm not the type of man to force love upon someone anymore. Love is two sided, both sides must put effort into a relationship for it to work and it's obvious that I'm the giver and you're just the receiver. You'll just throw away anything that I give you and that's one of the things I learned while sitting in prison for six years. Cherish everything that is golden to you because only a fool would throw away something so dear to one's heart."

His words burned holes through me, but I understood what he was saying and it hurt. Was it true? Would I really throw away his never ending love? I didn't know the answer. I heard my apartment door open and slowly close back, and that's when I knew I did want his love. I wouldn't throw away his affection, I want to cherish it just like he cherished me during those six years.

I ran to the front door, opening it then slamming it shut. I ran down the apartment steps, almost slipping on the icy steps. I saw his dark shadow walking slowly down the vacant street, my heart was racing at this point. I didn't have an idea what I was going to say but I knew it needed to be good. I slowed my pace down, taking this time to observe him. His head was hung low, hands in his pockets. His breath was showing then fading away into the cool November air.

"If you'll be the giver, I'll be more than a receiver. I'll be a taker, a holder, and I'll cherish you because you, Hunter Lee Stiles, are gold." I spoke the words with as much passion and love as I could and they were true.

He is truly golden. He may have a few dark spots, but nothing a little love couldn't fix. Hunter slowly turned around to face me, our bodies about five feet apart. We stared at each other for what felt like ages which was really a couple minutes, but I began to panic when he was silent for so long. Hunter just looked at me with dull green eyes and simply said, before walking off, "As a great poet once said, 'nothing gold can stay.'"

Chapter 47

Hunter

I walked away.

I had nothing left to say to her. If she really longed for my love then why did she hesitate when I expressed my feelings to her? I knew it was a long shot, going after her, since it's been six years and I'd done so much to hurt her, but honestly, I've changed. I did it for her and here I was walking away from the one I loved most.

I spent six years, practicing how I would win her over and I guess that's six years of my life I wouldn't get back. Some may say I should have taken her back and others will agree I did the right thing, but in the end, love will make you go crazy. It has this way of seeping into your heart, telling you that someone really loves you when your brain is telling you no. My heart told me to go after Cassandra even though my brain warned me about her and how I'll just end up heartbroken in the end.

Love also comes at the strangest of times. Just when you think you'll die alone with 69 cats, that certain someone comes along and says otherwise. I didn't mean to fall in the love with her at the time, she was just supposed to be another girl I would drop off at the warehouse and never see again but she caught my attention and she's had it for over six years. So yes, I could say I went crazy over the idea of "love."

In the dreams I had of us as a family in later years, I would wake her up by placing small kisses all over her delicate face. We would have one son and two daughters. Twins. I would let Cassie pick out our son's name. He would protect them when I wasn't home because if our daughters looked anything like Cassandra, they would need lots of protection; but I guess that's all rubbish now. I'd never marry Cassandra and have beautiful children with her, she'd never be Mrs. Stiles, and it saddens me to know this; but that's the truth, and sometimes we need to hear the truth. Even though it hurts like hell.

I was just now arriving home. Once I got out of jail, I flew straight to New York because that's where Cassie lived. It's just a small apartment with one bedroom, a bath, and a conjoined living room and kitchen.

I threw my keys down on the coffee table and went straight to my room. I grabbed my suitcase from the top shelf of my closet and started tossing my clothes and other items in it. There's no point of me staying here since the only reason I moved here was because of her.

Once I packed my small amount of clothes, I got online and looked up airline tickets back to London. I was ready to go home, even though there was no one there waiting for me, I was just ready to be back in my birth place. To be home.

Cassandra

I couldn't believe he just walked away like that. I just confessed my love back to him and he went and did this? It's obvious he waited for those six years to come and tell me that since he came straight to me once he was released, but I really thought he would take me back. It took a lot to do that, to forgive him that easily. He hurt me and my family and I knew it was the other him doing it, and I felt bad he had to go through that; but for him to just walk away like that hurts me inside.

Maybe it's for the better, maybe we weren't supposed to fall in love, if you even want to call it falling in love. Maybe we just weren't meant to be, but I wished he would have at least gave us a chance. I walked back up the ice wet steps and head for my apartment.

Once I was finally on the top step and had reached my door, I saw that it's slightly cracked open. I guess I didn't shut it on my way out since I was in such a big hurry. I opened the door and quickly shut it behind me so the cold air wouldn't get in. I started to pull off my coat, but I froze when I heard a smooth voice speak my name. I slowly turned around. I was shocked at who stood before me dressed in all black, hair slicked back. I breathlessly spoke, "Zach?"

Chapter 48

I stood before a man with jet black hair and a stubble of a beard.

His dark brown eyes stared back at me as I was in utter shock. His jawline defined his face, giving him this sexy aura about him. He looked the same from six years ago, just slightly older.

"Yes, Cassie, it's really me. Surprised?" He grinned, standing up straighter.

"I—What are you doing here?" I stuttered.

He just chuckled at me like I had told a funny joke, which I certainly hadn't.

"Oh, Cassandra. I see you haven't gotten any smarter since the last time I saw you." He cackled some more.

I was growing mad at the way he just told me I was stupid.

"Well you see, Cass, I came back for you."

My palms started to sweat and my breathing became irregular at his simple yet frightening words.

"No. How did you even survive?" I asked, not believing this was happening again.

My past was playing itself over but this time with a different psycho.

"Well I could have let myself die; but then I thought, well, Hunter will obviously go to jail for a very long time and you will go on with your life; and since everyone will think I died, nobody will suspect me to be the one to take you. It is the perfect plan."

My mouth fell agape. I couldn't believe this, this wasn't happening. It couldn't be. I had to get out of here. I turned around and quickly run for the door and went to grab it, but before I could a voice stopped me.

"I don't think you'll want to leave him behind."

I slowly turned around and saw Ben, my brother, standing beside Zach. He had a gun pointed to his head.

"Let him go," I demanded, walking closer.

"Now. Why would I do that?" Zach asked, putting the gun against Ben's forehead.

"Please stop. He has lost enough as it is," I argued.

"Oh, you mean his leg? Where Hunter shot him." He pointed to Ben's prosthetic leg.

"Yes," I said, trying to hold my coolness.

"What do you even want with us?" I snapped at him.

"Woah, now. Settle down," he told me, raising his hands up in defense.

"Well? What do you want?" I asked, eager to know.

"I simply want you." He locked gazes with me as an evil grin appears on his plump lips.

"Well you can't have me," I sternly told him while putting my hands on my hips.

"Oh really?" Zach pointed the gun at Ben's other leg, getting ready to pull the trigger.

"Stop!" I yelled, he put it down and my heartbeat came down.

"Good, now get over here." I didn't ask why, and I just obeyed.

Once I stood in front of the disgusting man, he pushed both me and Ben onto the couch. I hugged my younger brother, and he was lightly hugging me back. I knew it's just because he thinks he's a man now when in reality he's just a fourteen-year-old boy with raging hormones and a squeaky voice going through puberty.

"I love you," I whispered in his ear.

"I love you too," he told me.

"Awe, how sweet. Some brother-slash-sister love, how cute. Now cut it out!" he yelled, and we both jumped back.

"Now I want you to be quiet," he told us while he started digging around in a black bag.

After searching for a bit, he pulled out some rope and a duct tape. I started to scream but he just came over and slapped me across the face. It stung, I must say, but I didn't dare cry. I couldn't let him know how weak I am.

"Now you'll learn to keep your mouth shut." Zach pulled off a piece of tape and came over to me. He took it and taped my mouth shut then did the same to Ben and tied both our hands up. I couldn't believe this was happening.

After tying us up he lead us outside to an old black van that didn't have a single window in the back, which freaked me out because these are the kind of vans me and my friends call rape vans. It is awful but it's the truth. They're so sketchy looking.

He pushed me and Ben into the van, slamming the door shut behind him.

A thought came into my head. How did Ben get all the way up here in New York? Zach must have taken him, God I hope he didn't do anything to him.

The ride was long and very bumpy one. Once the van had come to a halt, the door opened seconds later. Zach pulled us out, throwing both of us on the ground. I let out a pained scream but it was muffled by the tape.

"Get up!" he yelled, pulling us up from the ground.

When I looked up to see where we were, all I saw was a large brick building. He pushed us by the back towards an alley. It was dark now, the November air slicing through us. The small space between the two brick buildings was wet and filled with trash.

Zach led us to a door, then he dug around in his pockets I'm guessing for a key. Once found he found it, he stuck it in the lock and let us in. We came face to face with a flight of stairs. After climbing them, we were met with a small apartment.

Zach turned on the lights, patting me on the back and announcing, "Welcome home."

Chapter 49

I couldn't believe Zach had taken Ben and got away with it and now had us both. Like, what are the odds?

It was currently 11 pm and Zach had handcuffed us and thrown us in a small room with one bed and a night stand that were next to each other. Ben had fallen asleep, his head resting in my lap. I was gazing down at my pinky finger where the name Ben is tattooed. I remembered getting it with Hunter at that shop where I think the girl's name was Storm. She had colored my hair and done my makeup before I got the small ink done. Just thinking of Hunter and how different he was back then made me realize why I hated him so much, but people change with time.

He changed in the past six years. I wish he was sweet back then like he is now but he's long gone, and there's nothing I could do about it. All I needed to be thinking about is how I'm going to get me and Ben out of this mess. I needed to figure out why Zach wants me.

I got up out of the bed, gently laying Ben's head on the pillow. He stirred in his sleep but didn't wake up. I walked over to the locked door and knocked on it softly, hoping Zach would open it. Seconds later, I heard footsteps padding towards the door. It opened and I saw his dark brown eyes staring into mine.

"What do you want?" he asked with no emotion in his voice.

"I need to talk to you."

He hesitated for a minute before opening the door all the way so I could get to the living room. He led me to sit on the couch, so I did. He took a seat across from me.

"Okay, I want you to tell me why I'm here."

He looked at me and started laughing. "You really are stupid," he told me. Yet again he had called me stupid right to my face.

"Will you please just be clear and tell me?" I yelled. I was tired and not in the mood for his bullshit. I just wanted to know the answer.

"I will but what I just don't get is how you haven't seen it already."

I felt dumb, okay, maybe I am dumb. What was I not getting? Why was I out of the loop? "I have no idea what you're talking about."

"Tell me what you do know." He raised a brow.

Well, I knew practically nothing.

"Tell me what you know about me."

I had to think because to be honest, I knew hardly anything.

"Well I thought your were a sweet, gay makeup artist then you ended up being a psycho and tried to kill us both by driving us off a bridge!" I yelled at him, but he just laughed it off.

"True, what else?"

Blank. That was what my brain looked like, I had nothing else. "I can't think of anything else," I said truthfully.

"Why do you think Hunter picked you in the first place?" he asked me.

"I don't know," I said.

"Hunter's job was to pick up young, stupid, pretty girls and bring them to the warehouse to be sold as entertainment to wealthy men. And you were no exception, but Hunter saw something else in you, something he hadn't ever seen in any other girl who walked through that door, and I think I finally figured you out." I was clueless as to where this was going.

"You, Cassandra, have something that none of the other girls had and it had an effect on Hunter." Where was this going? What effect? I kept thinking.

"You, Cassie, are innocent. Pure, like a newborn baby but on top of being all those things you're also a woman. A very beautiful, sexy woman that men can't wait to get their hands on. My and Hunter's lives have been hectic and troublesome when yours was practically a piece of cake, a stroll in the park compared to ours and he loved the fact that you hadn't yet seen the cruel world firsthand. He wanted to protect you, that's why he wanted you so badly, Cassandra."

It sort of made sense but I was still lost. Why would he want to protect me so bad? And I had seen the cruel world firsthand, not as bad as them, but I had.

"Okay, so why did you take me and my brother?" I asked, ready to know the answer.

"Well you have the same effect on me as well, I want to protect you. Keep you safe from the world. Plus, you're hot so that's a bonus." He grinned. "But I'm not like Hunter, I don't want to keep you pure." A devilish smirk played on his features and I was afraid as to where this was going. "But you might want to keep it down unless you want your brother involved."

My hands were shaking at this point. He can't be serious, can he?

"Don't be scared, I'll be gentle." He started to move closer to me, but I just run to the kitchen with him following closely behind. "Don't even try to hide, Cassie. I'll just find you in the end."

I was currently under the kitchen table, gripping a butter knife I had saw laying on the kitchen counter. Lame, I know but it's the first thing I saw, and I guess it's better than nothing.

"Come out, come out," Zach sang in the most creepy-sounding voice.

"It won't hurt... much," he said the last part under his breath but I still heard it.

"It's not like I'm going to try and kill you again, I was stupid back then, I'll admit."

"I see you, Cassie," he whispered right beside my ear.

I screamed and jumped out from under the table and darted back to the living room.

"There's nowhere to go so just come willingly and it will be better for the both of us."

I was stuck, there was nowhere to go, like he said. Zach stood at the kitchen doorway, smirking at my failure to escape. "Maybe it won't be as bad as you think," he told me, walking closer.

I just shot him my best disgusted look.

Hunter

After I was done packing, I sat down in my small living room, turning on the TV and flipping through the channels. There was a cooking show on and some kids' shows, nothing I wanted to watch so I just settled on the news.

"A young boy and his sister previously kidnapped by Hunter Stiles over six years ago have gone missing, again. Ben, the fourteen year old was taken from his home two days ago. His parents had tried to get in contact with his older sister, Cassandra, who now lives in New York but failed to do so. Police went to her apartment only to find no sign of her. A note was found left on the kitchen table. It read, 'HELP. A man with dark hair and brown eyes is kidnapping us. He goes by the name Zach. — Ben' The letter was written very sloppily, as if jotted down in a hurry."

I couldn't believe what I was hearing. This can't be! I can't let her go through this again. I grabbed my keys off the counter, getting ready to turn off the TV and leave but the reporter wasn't done yet.

"A neighbor of Cassandra's saw a man, wearing all black, pulling up in a black van and leaving with two people. He believed that it was Ben and Cassandra. If you have any information on this case, please call 1800-crime-stoppers." With that, I turned it off and headed out the door.

I got in my car, pulling out of the drive way drove towards Cassie's apartment.

Chapter 50

Cassandra

My hands were shaking at my sides as my mind raced as to what I needed to do. Zach was walking over to me with a devilish grin. I turned to unlock the door but before I could, he grabbed me by my forearms and pulled me to him.

"Did you really think you could escape that easily?" I just shook in his arms as he held my wrists in a tight grip. I knew I couldn't leave Ben, but I also knew Zach wouldn't hurt him if he wanted me to come back.

"No,' I blankly said as tears started to blur my vision. I didn't want to cry, I really didn't, but I just couldn't help the tears from silently down my cheeks.

"That's what I thought. Now, be a good girl and follow me to my room quietly," he told me, slowly leaving a trail of kisses down my neck.

I just shivered under his cold lips as he pulled me down the hallway. I dragged my feet, hoping to buy myself some time, but it's obvious Zach wasn't buying it. He just tugged my arms harder.

He opened a door and turned on a light. I'm guessing this was his bedroom. There's a queen-sized bed in the middle of the room with a nightstand on either side of it and a few more pieces of wooden furniture sitting around the medium-sized room. He pushed me over to the bed and told me to sit, so I did.

"I have a surprise for you." He smirked and walked over to a dresser and dug around in it till he found what he was looking for.

"These will look so good on you," Zach told me as he held up a pair of metal pink handcuffs.

I began to shake again and planned on making a dart for the door, but before I could, he's standing in front of me with a grin plastered on his hard features.

"Now be a really good girl and let me put these on you."

I looked at him with pure disgust and said, "Like hell." I tried run away but he just grabbed me by the waist and threw me onto the ground. I was shocked as all the air in my lungs came flying out. I lay there as my backbones ached.

"Now, now, Cassie. You wouldn't want to wake Ben."

He was a horrible person, just plain disgusting. I stayed quiet and just let the tears fall even more.

"That's what I thought," he grabbed me by the waist and hooked his arms under my legs and carried me to the bed. "Now grab onto the headboard," he demanded.

I looked at the metal bars, knowing exactly what he had in mind. "No," I breathed out. I would not be giving up this easy, not without a fight at least.

"What did you just say?" he growled, moving his face closer to mine.

I just leaned back further into the soft pillow, not wanting him this close to me. "I think you heard me," I fire back.

He just chuckled while shaking his head. "Oh, stupid, stupid Cassandra. When will you ever learn?" Zach brought his face back down to where mine was. "You don't know who you are messing with."

Before I could even comprehend what was happening, he had slapped me across the face, making my left cheek sting in pain. I cried out for him to stop, but he just repeated his previous actions over and over till I was screaming his name to stop.

"Save your screaming for later, sweetheart." And with that he got up and left the room.

I was more than happy for him leaving, but I was also worried that he went to go get Ben. But to my little prayer I said after he left, Zach came back alone with only what looked like a glass of water in hand.

"I brought you something," he whispered, nearing me with the drink, but something told me that the small cup held more than just water.

"What is it?" I dared to ask.

"Nothing too special." He smirked, handing me the drink. "Now, drink up," he cooed.

I closed my mouth tightly, not daring any of that to get into my system. I could not even tell what in Go's name it would do to me.

"Drink up, flunitranzepam is waiting to work its magic."

Before I could understand the drug he was referring to, I had already drank half the cup and Zach was trying his best to force more down on me. Once most of the "water" was down, he sat beside me, waiting for something to happen. I remembered my father speaking once of this drug. It's supposed to make you feel drunk, well that's how he explained it to me.

"Soon you'll be higher than a kite, and I can finally have my way with you," Zach whispered in my ear then began to trace patterns on my exposed stomach.

Once he pulled my top up, I shivered under his touch, trying to picture myself elsewhere, anywhere for that matter, but I couldn't rid his mocking smirk from my brain.

"Your skin is going to feel so good under mine, Cass."

I cringed at the nickname, this really was happening and I'm just hoping the drug would knock me out, maybe even kill me because I was not really for sure if I wanted to wake up after this.

"I've wanted this for a very long time now, I've needed this. I've needed you, Cassie, and now you're finally mine."

Tears were beginning to fill my closed eyes, everything I've ever wanted has been taken away from me. Even the smallest of things, like waiting for marriage or at least waiting till I was ready. I hardly knew this disgusting excuse for a man, now in minutes I'd be enduring a whole new feeling. A feeling which should be shared with someone you love, not a horny bastard who can't keep his greedy hands off young girls. If I ever have children, I hope they won't ever throw away their first time or get forced into it. I'd never felt more scared and nervous in my life. I could only hope that the drug would rid my brain of this night.

"It won't be long now."

And sure enough, I started to feel my muscles weaken and my mind seemed to not comprehend things as fast as normal. I felt someone's cold fingers struggling to undo my pants button. I didn't even have the energy to push away the person doing it even though I knew it's Zach. I could see his tan skin working to pull them down now. My body was screaming for me to move or to do anything as his cold fingers slowly went to pull the lacy undergarments off.

"Don't be afraid, I won't bite," he whispered in my ear, and then a dark sinister laugh filled the room.

My brain kept reminding me how after this night, nothing would ever be the same. I wanted so badly to just get up and run away with Ben but I knew it was too late, far too late now. I made a short prayer, asking God to just kill me now and let Ben leave untouched, but in the back of my head I knew it would take a miracle for that to happen. It seemed that this world we live in only grants wishes or prayers from time to time, hardly ever for that matter.

I closed my eyes, trying to escape this room and the horrible man in it. When I opened my eyes, the sweater I was wearing was now ripped into pieces and Zach was throwing it to the ground. I was left in only my underwear and bra as the beautiful yet disgusting man hovered above me.

"You're even more beautiful than I thought," he whispered in my ear.

I shivered as tears brimmed my eyes, wanting to fall, but it didn't even feel like I had the energy to cry. As pathetic as that sounds, but that drugged-up drink he gave me had really started working in the last few minutes. I was almost thankful for it, and I was hoping the drugged drink would rid this night I was sure to remember. I really hoped I do die. I tried one last time to kick him off of me, but it's no use. The drug was in full effect now. I couldn't even lift my legs. I could feel them but I just couldn't begin to move them. It's a very odd and depressing feeling.

Zach pulled his shirt over his head which exposed his chest full of tattoos. I couldn't even begin to tell what most of them were, his whole front was covered in them.

"Like what you see?"

I wanted to slap him for even thinking I liked his body. I didn't. Not one fiber in me liked anything that had to do with him.

"Come on, babe. Don't give me the silent treatment."

So that's exactly what I did. I closed my eyes, feeling light headed and wanting sleep, maybe this was death calling. Maybe if I just fall asleep, I'd never wake up again.

"You're going to love this, and if you don't, at least I will." It was the last thing I heard.

Hunter

Once I pull onto the highway, I headed straight for Cassandra's apartment even though I knew she wouldn't be there. I drove thirty over the speed limit, not really giving a shit if I got caught or not. I couldn't believe Zach took Cassandra. I thought that bastard was dead. He was supposed to die.

I pulled Cassie out and left his sorry arse for a reason. He tried to kill her, and now he had come back from the dead to seek revenge? But why would he take her? Yes, I knew he probably fantasized over her, and I don't blame him, she is perfect and so beautiful and pure; but I'd come to realize neither one of us really deserve her. I love her so much but it's clear now how bad of an impact I left on her, and every day for the last six years I had wished I could have never done those terrible things and treated her so poorly. It broke my heart to know she was with yet another horrible man who wanted to do who knows what to her so I must find her.

Even though I couldn't take back my actions, I could prevent more bad ones from occurring in her life.

I pulled into her apartment complex parking lot to see at least ten cop cars surrounding the building. "Great, just great." I thought on what I should do, and a thought popped into my head.

I knew it's long shot, but I had no other options. I got out my phone and dialed Cassandra's number. It rang four times before going straight to voicemail. "Wonderful, just wonderful," I thought to myself as I was scrolling through my phone, trying to think of anything I could do.

An app caught my attention. How could I have been this stupid? After getting out of jail and finding Cassandra and once she gave me her number, I put a tracker on her phone. I went onto the app pushing onto Cassie's number, and it gave me directions to where she was. I quickly pulled out from the lot and headed back on the highway.

I knew I should have called the cops, telling them I know where she was, but I just could't bring myself to do it. I needed to settle this with Zach. Alone.

"I'm coming for you, baby," I whispered to myself and sped down the interstate.

Cassandra

Tears fell and stained my cheeks as pain shot through my lower region. I cried for it all to stop but nobody heard my pleas except the man causing the pain. I felt awful, disgusting, and dirty. My brain was overloaded with so many emotions, I didn't even know what to think. I hoped, praying that the drug would ease any pain I was to feel, but it's obvious it doesn't numb you that way.

My vision was blurry, I was not sure if it's from the tears or if my vision was just off from the drink. I squeezed my eyes shut tightly as the pain became unbearable. I screamed for him to stop but my cries didn't even phase him one bit. I tried to kick, thrash, or do anything to get him off, but my body wouldn't move. It's like I weighed a thousand pounds and I just couldn't pick my own weight up.

I think my father was wrong about feeling drunk. It didn't feel like being drunk. It's a scary feeling, not being able to move and only being allowed to see everything that's going on around you, but if there was a fire, you would just burn away to ashes at this point. I wished there was a fire and I would just disappear, escape this cruel world, leaving behind my brother—the only one who truly cares about me, I have no one else. I hadn't seen my mother and father since I moved up here to New York, and it's been five years. Hunter didn't even care, heck, he left me after I confessed my love to him. He just left, leaving me standing there like an idiot, and Ben would just forget me anyways.

"I love you so much," he spoke as the pain came again.

I wanted to cry but I had no tears left so I just winced in pain and stared at the clock on the wall, watching as the time passed. After staring it down for a straight ten minutes, the tears returned stronger than ever. The pain appeared, even more unbearable than before, but I couldn't move or scream and I could hardly see. The room began to spin, sending me into a confused daze. My body ached in places I didn't know could hurt, red spots, and other things I didn't know litter the bed sheets. I shut my eyes as the world around me still spun. The pressure and stinging I once felt had faded, but it was still there lingering around. I didn't dare open my eyes for two reasons: one, I didn't even want to see Zach, and two, I didn't think I could even open them. My body felt drained from any energy I had before this happened.

Slowly, I started to feel tired and like I just couldn't take fighting the sleep any longer so as I slowly fell into another world. I heard a familiar voice screaming my name but not even the raspy voice could bring me to open my eyes.

Hunter

I banged on the door, practically beating it down, before I kicked it in, giving up on anyone answering. I held the gun tightly in my sweaty palms, my heartbeat running wild.

"Cassandra! Zach!" I yelled through the house, but no one seemed to hear. I tried to open a door, but it's locked. She must be in there. I banged and beat on the door, yelling at Zach to let me in; but before anyone answered, I kick the door in.

I was shocked at who I saw with wide eyes staring back at me. Once I entered the room, I saw Ben, Cassie's little brother. I knew he probably hated me for all I'd done to him, but I could only hope he didn't realize who I am.

"Hunter?" he asked, backing away from me.

Well, shit. Of course he would remember, why the heck did I even think he wouldn't? "Yeah, it's me. Now, where's Cassandra?" I asked, looking around the room.

"S-she left earlier to talk to Zach but never returned."

With that said, I ran out of the room, Ben following close behind, and stopped at a door. "Is this his room?" I pointed towards a wooden door. Ben just shrugged, not knowing the answer. I didn't even try kicking the door down, I just shot the lock and it gave up. I run in, telling Ben to stay back.

Tears rimmed my eyes at the sight in front of me. Cassandra lay completely naked on the bed with her hands cuffed to the headboard. The sheets along with her petite body were placed on sheets spotted with blood and a few articles of clothing. I run over to her, forcing my eyes to look anywhere but her beautiful body. I knew it wasn't the time to be thinking such dirty things. I took off my jacket and laid it over her.

"Baby, wake up. It's me, Hunter," I cooed in her ear, brushing away the hair from her face.

She stirred, lightly mumbling some words I couldn't quite figure out.

"Well, well. If it isn't Hunter Stiles himself."

I glared at Zach as he smirked down at Cassie. "What the hell did you do?" I yelled, gesturing to her naked body. I knew what he did to my Cassandra, but I just couldn't believe it.

"What the hell do you think I did?" He laughed.

My teeth clenched at his words. I couldn't believe this.

"I might have let you join if I knew you were in town."

He was sick, just plain sick in the head. "You're disgusting." I spat.

"And you aren't? The whole reason behind bringing the girls to the warehouse was to do this! And you were the main man, you brought in the most girls."

I felt sick at the horrible memory. "That was over six years ago, Zach. I've changed! I went to jail and guess what? It changed me! Maybe you should try it!" I fired back while moving closer to him.

"I would rather die than rot away in prison." He stepped even closer to me, I held the gun tightly. "And if I were in jail, I wouldn't have been able to do her." He pointed to my not-so-innocent Cass.

"You're disgusting!" I yelled at his cocky grin and push him back.

He stepped forward, recovering quickly from the shove, and started swinging punches at me. One second I had him pinned down, the next he had me. We went on like this for five minutes or more before I had him back down on the ground with the gun pointed right in the middle of his forehead.

"Do it, Hunter. I dare you," he tells me, the grin never leaving his face. "Do it, prove to the world that deep down you never changed. Not one bit."

My hands shake as my finger set on the trigger.

"I'm a dead man anyway."

Sirens filled the air.

***

I glanced back over to the doorway where Ben stood with wide eyes. Before I knew what was happening, Zach had grabbed the gun from my hands, but he didn't have the gun pointed towards me.

The shot fired, and I jump back from the sound. When I looked over my shoulder, Zach lay lifeless on the ground. I was beyond shocked, I couldn't believe he did that, but I didn't really feel bad. I'm glad he's dead. Bad as that sounds, but he hurt my Cassandra.

At just the mention of her name, I jolted up from my spot on the ground and run over to her. I searched for the keys to the cuffs and found them laying on the dresser. I quickly unlocked them and held her tightly in my arms.

"Baby, wake up." I sat down on the ground, moving the hair away from her pale face and made sure to keep the jacket covering her. I knew she would kill me if she knew I had saw her naked, but that's not important right now.

"Open your eyes, let me see them," I began to tear up from her not responding. What the heck did Zach do to her? Did he drug her? I pushed the thought away and rest my head on her neck, placing small kisses all around the skin.

I felt like a sap. I knew she'd wake up, but I needed to hear her voice now and see her green eyes get lost in mine. I need her, I truly do love her.

Right when I was beginning to give up on her, her lips parted and her eyes opened. The first words that slipped from her pink lips being, "Where's Ben?"

Epilogue

Cassandra

Eleven months. That's how long it had been since the incident with Zach. Eleven months since the last time mine and my brother's life was threatened. Eleven months since the day I saw Hunter Stiles. It took almost a year for me to realize how naïve I was for ever believing that somewhere in my heart, I held feelings for the man who kidnapped me and my brother.

Did you know he shot my little brother's leg and endangered my life countless times? I do admit that my thoughts and actions were foolish, but I was young and scared. What could I have done? I felt like I'd grown up too fast. I probably have. I looked into my eyes and felt as if I'd aged a hundred years in such a short time.

I really was slowly ruining my life with every feeling I gained for that man, and I knew it. Somewhere in my mind, I knew I was. I'm only human, and humans are so delicate and fragile. One jump, we die. One step too far, we die. One single bullet, and we die.

Just like that. Yet, I pretended to be blind to the wrecking ball heading straight for my life.

Zach and Hunter, they both ruined and changed my life in a way I couldn't bear to think about. I lost my friends, my family, and my job. Because of them, my work found out about my little date with Lee. And before I knew, it was Hunter who was the reason for all of this. I got fired. I guess I failed to remember the policy about dating your patient. It was strictly against the rules, forbidden and no exceptions. But the more something is forbidden, the more we want it.

My family, well I didn't really lost them, but I sure don't get many phone calls from them. There's only few every now and again, but honestly, I don't blame them. I don't blame them for not inviting me for thanksgiving, no. I don't blame them for anything. I get that they don't want to bring up bad memories, especially when I am the worst memory of them all. Nobody even knows where to start a conversation with me. They're too afraid they'll set me off. Something that has happened one too many times. I'd be lying if I said that it didn't bother me much. But it's true that I don't really know what to feel.

My mother still calls to check up on me every couple of weeks, and Ben sends me a text, saying how he wished I would move back home; but I'd already explained to them that the seventeen-year-old girl they knew was long gone. And she isn't coming back. I couldn't live there. Too many bad memories, even though I am a bad memory myself. But it would more bad memories colliding together well. I didn't want to feel more pain than I'd experienced already. I needed to start a new life and make new memories. Memories that would hopefully overthrow the old ones.

My friends have had other plans. Hanging out with a twenty-four year old along with two-month-old baby wasn't exactly the party of their lifetime. Nor was I the ideal person to ask to join them on a movie night or a totally awesome nightclub that just opened a few days ago. I guess I couldn't blame them either. I'm now a mother, which means that my apartment reeks of diapers, unwashed bottles, and dirty bed sheets. There's also the useless dummies littered across the floor and the occasional dishes that are overdue for washing. Add, one more milk-splashed bib and this place becomes a five-star hotel for any critter and insect.

Now you know what my elegant apartment looks like. You get to find out who the fairest of them all is. There's my poofy hair, mucky clothes, pungent feet, and malodorous breath. I don't even remember the last time I slept through the night without being woken up.

Madison is very talented at crying, but she makes up for her little flaw with her perfections. Her soft, dark hair and smooth, olive skin. She's beautiful and amazing in every way possible. I would never change what happened to me because of Madison.

Damn, I sound like a typical teenage girl that's usually found in cliché stories.

I've learned a lot in these past eleven months. One of them being the most frequently asked question. What is the definition of love? There goes the typical teenage girl again. I'd asked myself this question many times and I still don't have my answer but I am starting to get a gist of what it may be. I know all the wrong meanings, for me anyway.

Love isn't falling for someone just because they look like the hottest person imaginable. Love isn't all about sex or lustful thoughts. Love isn't the same as an infatuation. Love, to me, is about accepting and understanding that special person in your life. Accepting them for who they are, even after you've seen their darkest times. Understanding them, helping them face their demons.

This is your cue to stop and think, "Did she forgive her kidnapper and end up marrying him even after telling us she hasn't seen him in eleven months? This is the typical *teenage-ish* girl who got knocked up by some random guy!"

The answer to that is no, I am not the typical, cliché girl. At least, I hope so, but no. I didn't marry my kidnapper, but I am seeing someone. I've seen him and his darkest times. But he hasn't hurt me so far, no.

Anyway, I won't focus on the bad. Instead, I'll tell you how we met, since that's almost always an interesting story. The way we met, where do I start? I was in labor, in excruciating pain, driven to the point of screaming for this child to "get out of me." I was desperate, and desperate times call for desperate measures. I knocked on one of my neighbour's—his—apartment door, hoping for one of the few kind people in this world to drive me to the hospital. I've seen him around. I had have a few conversations with him and he seemed sweet. Wasn't bad looking, either. Oh, okay. I knew that wasn't technically the exact day we met but do you want to listen to a funny story or to a boring exchange of hellos in a coffee shop? Actually, that was rather funny, no, this is funnier. Shut up and listen.

It took what seemed like the most painful and longest minutes of my life before he answered the door, ready to help the screaming woman on the other side and to do whatever task I needed him to fulfill. A little dramatic but hey, it was accurate.

Within minutes, he was carrying me, still to this day I wonder how with my whale of a belly, and after arriving at the local hospital I figured he would just drop me off; but he was kind enough to come in and help me while I was sent to a room with nurses filling the area. Told you he was one of the few kind human species in this world.

One of the nurses asked if I had anybody I would like in the room with me but I said no. Why the hell would I want an acquaintance in a room where my child was going to pop out at any minute?

So, I was alone. Except for the few nurses and one doctor, of course, but seven painful hours later, Madison was born. I was filled with the joy most mothers have when their child enters the world for the first time. It was oh so gloriously—

The nurse interrupted my joy by opening her damn mouth. She said, "There's a man waiting outside, asking if he could come in." A harmless statement which I said no to, but it changed my life. This time for good.

I thought he had come back, Hunter that is, but I remembered Hunter had moved back to London. Good for him. After agreeing to let the person because of my curiosity, I was a little surprised as to who it was. My neighbor, the one who drove me there, who also belonged to the endangered species of kind people, had waited outside for seven hours just to make sure I was okay. Plus, he wanted to see the baby; but nevertheless, that's how our little relationship came to be.

He's perfect, even with every flaw, scar, burn, and mark that scattered in his body. And even though I've been to hell and back, I've learned that there is a hope for this world. After all, I'm happy. And I have my happily ever after.

The End

Can't get enough of Hunter and Cassandra?
Make sure you sign up for the author's blog to
find out more about them!

Get these two bonus chapters and more
freebies when you sign up at
http://alexayers.org/!

Here is a sample from another story you may enjoy:

THE BAD GIRL
and
THE GOOD BOY

K A R L A   L U N A

1: Some Bad News

• Evelyn Jo •

"Do you think he's dead or unconscious?"

I turned to look at Drake, who had his hand over his chin, skeptically looking at the motionless middle-aged man sprawled on the ground.

We were on our way to go get some delicious food when we found this guy in an alleyway nearby. He was actually one of the guys that owed us money for giving him a few *special* things. He had a business suit on, but his tie – which used to be light blue – was now covered in dirt and what seemed to be dry blood. So obviously, this had caught our attention since something bad must've happened to him. I mean, there had to be a reason he was here, like this.

Suddenly, Drake kicked the guy without any hesitation. He kicked him *hard*, and right in the stomach, making the guy roll over to his side. We all stood in silence for a few seconds, as the other two guys from our group – Ian and Darrel – inched closer to hear the man, in case he made any human sound at all. The man then groaned after a couple of moments, and Drake gave an approving look with a slight nod.

"Unconscious, all right. Still alive, but barely." He then walked around the man, his hands linked together behind him, as he seemed to be deep in thought. I wanted to roll my eyes at him, but all I did was smile a little at how cute he was actually being right now. "What should we do with this guy then?"

"I say we kill him," Ian immediately said, not missing a single beat. He shrugged right afterwards, as if it was no big deal that we would be killing a guy that already seemed to be on his deathbed by now.

"Psh, I say, we take out everything he has that is actually valuable, and then dump the helpless body in that Dumpster," Darrel suggested, as if it were obvious that it was the best idea ever conceived. He also pointed to the huge, green Dumpster right in front of us.

"Okay, Darrel's idea it is." Drake didn't even think twice about it. He motioned for Ian and Darrel to get to work, as he turned and stared right at me. I bit my lip and crossed my arms over my chest just as he came up to me to put his arm around my shoulders. "Cold?" he asked me.

I shook my head, watching Ian grab the guy by the arms and pull him up in a sitting position, while Darrel checked all of his pockets – finding a watch, a wallet, and some tickets.

"Wrestling tickets!?" Darrel yelled excitedly, as he and Ian high-fived each other. I couldn't help but laugh at the two idiots. Good thing there were actually four tickets, though. We all loved going to wrestling tournaments considering these guys wrestled too, and even took the time to show *me* a few moves, which was actually a lot of fun.

Coincidence that there were enough tickets for all of us? I think not.

"Scared?" I scoffed at Drake's question, just as he slid his hand to rest on my waist, pulling me closer so our stomachs could touch. He grabbed my face and gently pushed my wavy, brown hair away so that he could clearly see me.

"I don't even think we should be doing this," I honestly told him. "We just saw him here… I mean, sure he owes us money, but what if we get into trouble when we *technically* didn't do any damage to him?"

"Oh, Eve," Drake smirked, lightly pinching my chin as I moved my head away, raising one eyebrow at him. "You always make it sound so difficult. You've been in this group for quite a while now. You shouldn't question what we do with the people that don't understand the consequences. Like this guy, clearly."

I thought about it right then. What we did to people was way, way worse, sometimes, but I couldn't help but wonder who did this. Or if the guy actually did something to himself before we got to him.

"I always wondered…" Ian then came up to us, eating some French fries from a white paper bag. I gave him a disgusted look. *Where the hell did he find those? In the Dumpster?* "How come we hardly called our 'little group' a gang?"

"If you want to call it that, then fine, whatever. Doesn't really matter." Drake turned back to me, and then lightly kissed my forehead. I smiled as I felt his soft, warm lips on me. "Now, let's bail." He grabbed my hand, and then we all walked out of the alleyway together.

I've been with this gang ever since I was in the 10th grade. Now, I was in my senior year, which means I've been with these guys for about two years now. I had reasons why I decided to join their criminal gang. But it was a very touchy subject for me, so I always kept it a secret. And Drake was the only one who really knew about my past. But hey, the past was in the past. It made us who we are today. And the bad stuff will continue to haunt us no matter what. But sometimes, we just had to forget it all – because now, the future is nearer, and it is actually more important.

Anyway (sorry, sometimes I get all deep and shit), what we actually did was break a few laws here and there – do drugs, rob, and hurt people, if we thought it was necessary to do so. Basically, we did anything a *good* and *innocent* kid wouldn't dare do.

Drake Lancaster was the eldest. He was 19, and out of high school, known as the leader of the gang. He was also my boyfriend ever since I started hanging out with him and the other two. He had dark eyes and short, dark hair. He was also the one who had saved me from my past misery, and showed me his rather *interesting* way of living.

Then, there were Ian Cohen and Darrel Ivanova. Those two, you could tell apart from their looks since Ian had light brown hair and light green eyes, while Darrel had blond hair and dark blue eyes. But their personalities were very alike. They were the jokesters and the more lovable ones. But don't let that always fool you, because like us, they were complete hell once you messed with them.

I was clearly the only girl in the gang. I went by the name Evelyn Jo. I was more of the feisty type, having a mischievous attitude that was actually serious sometimes, which was usually when I decided to get tough on people. I did a few bad things, and was taught how to fight and rebel. I had long, silky brown hair with big blue eyes, and was thin with olive skin. I had looked innocent once, but all of that had obviously changed.

That was the whole group right there. We were the type of people parents warned their kids about, but of course, not a lot of people knew who we were since we always kept our faces hidden while we were doing something that might involve jail if we ever got caught.

Drake was the only one who's ever been in juvie though, for four years, when he was just a bit younger. The rest of us have not yet done anything that would've sent us to juvie, mostly because we weren't planning on getting caught. But who knew? Anything could happen.

"Ugh."

I sipped my Coke and looked up at Drake, who was looking down at his phone with a frustrated look on his face.

"We gotta go," he said, putting his phone back in his pocket.

"Whoa, whoa! Right now?" Ian asked, looking up from his French fries, which were stacked up on top of each other like the game Jenga.

"Psh, yeah, we're kind of in the middle of something here?" Darrel shook his head at Drake. But Drake only slammed his fist on the table and got up. He pointed at the two guys.

"If you guys aren't in the car in 45 seconds, I'm fucking leaving you here." He was off after that, leaving right through the back door.

I knew then that we had a drug deal coming our way, which would explain Drake's harsh attitude. He hated missing a deal because of us. Or rather, because of Ian and Darrel here.

I deeply sighed, grabbed my jacket, and stood up from the table. I stopped to look at the two morons, who pretty much seemed way more excited than a little kid on Christmas morning. Typical Ian and Darrel.

Then I did the only thing that would wipe those happy faces off immediately. I grabbed a French fry from the bottom and yanked it off, making the whole tower fall... along with their pretty faces.

"Evelyn!" they both yelled in unison, getting glares and weird stares from the people around us. I only looked back and glared at them, mentally telling them to mind their own damn business.

"Get your asses outside and in the car, unless you want a pissed off Drake smashing your heads against the trunk."

A loud groan was heard all the way from where I was seated in the car. Drake suggested we leave this one to him, so we could go home right afterwards. But I admit, I hated being left out. My fist needed something to punch right about now. What?! I always had the need to, even when I was pretty calm.

Hmm... I pursed my lips in boredom. *Maybe I could play that one zombie game on my phone. I do have to beat that one level after all.*

"Hey, guys, is my phone back there? I need to..." I cut myself off when I turned to see the two morons sprawled across the back seats with their mouths hanging wide open as they practically slept like babies. They snored and Ian even had his fist halfway inside Darrel's mouth. Pathetic. A little gross. And stupidly hilarious.

I shrugged and jammed my fist on the horn button, earning yelps and grunts right after the loud beeping was made. The car moved as they both woke up, and I even heard one of them hit himself hard on the ceiling of the car. I just smiled innocently as if I hadn't done a single thing.

"What the hell, Evelyn?" Ian asked, just as Drake slid in with four large packs of money. He gave me one, and then tossed the guys their share.

"Why did you beat the guy up?" I asked, remembering the loud groans from earlier. Who knew, maybe the guy was making Drake pretty mad and I bet he regretted it a lot by now.

"What?" Drake asked with a confused expression. I raised my eyebrows at him until he realized what I had meant. "Oh, the guy just slipped on some wet mud, that's all."

"Let me guess. You just laughed, like, a lot. And then, you didn't even think about helping him up. You just grabbed the money and left."

He just nodded as if it wasn't a big deal.

"Pretty much, yeah." He started the engine and drove off. I didn't miss that smirk on his lips though. "You know me so well, babe."

"I know you so well... because I totally would've done the same thing!" I laughed and playfully slapped his arm.

He only chuckled at me. "By the way, why'd you press the horn? I didn't take *that* long."

"First, you lasted ten minutes and you know how impatient and bored I get in only ten minutes. Then, I decided I wanted to play a zombie game and remembered my phone was in my bag in the back, but these two were sleeping."

Drake glanced at the guys from the rearview mirror and sighed. I think they were sleeping again...

"Doesn't quite surprise me," he said. "Let's go home now. This was a pretty busy day."

We got to our house in less than fifteen minutes. We all lived together in a one-story house that had two bedrooms. It was painted light brown and black, and we did keep it very clean due to Drake's slight OCD.

Ian and Darrel shared a bedroom, while Drake and I shared another. We had separate beds, since we never really went that far with each other – even with being together this long. I was a virgin, but I guess most people wouldn't expect that from someone like me. Although, it was a probability, since I was really good at playing with boys. Drake let me share his bed sometimes (for some reason, not quite willingly). And I have to admit, it was very fun to do. But that was all I ever did. I was a criminal, yes, but I wasn't sexually driven or anything. And I was glad Drake wasn't like one of the asses who demanded sex, or thought it was the only way into a relationship. He really was a good guy deep down, even with all the bad stuff he's involved in.

I opened the front door to our house with a small smile on my face, and realized how tired I actually felt right then. Once I looked up though, my heart practically stopped beating at the sight in front of me.

There, standing *right there* in front of us, was my high school principal, the supervisor of the whole district, a guy from social services, and some other guy that looked like a cop in disguise. Well, to me he looked like it.

Shit. This could not be good.

Wait, how the hell did they even get in here? *Ugh...* Ian must've left the damn door open. *Again.* We seriously had to stop letting him be the last person to leave the house.

"I swear she did it," Ian immediately said, his arms raised in defense as he pointed at me.

"It was *aaaaall* her," Darrel mimicked, pushing me forward.

I quickly turned to glare at them both.

Yeah, nice to know you guys have my back!

"U-um... what's going on?" I asked in the most angelic voice I could muster.

"Evelyn Jo," my principal said, and as always, he never failed to look *so* happy (note the sarcasm, please). "We have some very important news to tell you."

"W-what is it? Am I in trouble?"

I always asked that, even though I already knew the answer to it. But hey, maybe – and just *maybe* – one day, it would be different.

Ha! Good one, Evelyn.

Okay, it was no time to joke around at that moment.

"Well, that and," the supervisor spoke up this time, "we are here to tell you that you will be moving schools. Again."

What? No, no, no. There's no other school left in the district!

Okay, so maybe wrecking the principal's car *and* setting almost half of the school on fire wasn't really a good idea, now that I really thought about it. But still, I must admit, it was pretty damn awesome!

"Considering you have no legal guardian and you're under the age of 18…"

"Whoa, whoa! She has me," Drake chimed in as he pressed his hand to his chest, giving them both a hard look. "I'm 19. Besides, she's turning 18 in just a couple of months. I can actually take full custody of her."

"Sorry, sir, we meant legal guardians, not pretentious boyfriends," the supervisor continued. "It's true you can take full custody, but I honestly think you're the one causing her to behave in such a terrible, rebellious way – which is why the police will now keep a close eye on you and your little friends over here." He looked at Ian and Darrel almost disapprovingly. "I mean, we could take you to jail, but we have no proof of the things you might've done in the past. *Yet.*"

That's when Ian and Darrel practically started hiding and backing away as if they weren't even involved in this whole conversation. But then, they cursed under their breath when they bumped into some police officers that had appeared right by the door.

"What the he—"

"No comment," the supervisor said in a stern voice, interrupting Drake, who seemed ready to pounce on him right then and there with the look he was giving off.

"So," the principal started, "we will have to take you away, Evelyn. But you have two choices." He made a stupid, dramatic silence and I realized I *also* wanted to pounce on someone… "First choice is the Orphanage."

What?

No... I didn't want to go back there. I had to live there ever since I was little, considering I had never met my birth parents. But those people at the Orphanage treated me so bad. I thought they were supposed to be good and nice to us, but they never were. It got me mad. *So* mad I just…

I clenched my fists and tried to stop thinking about that cruel, evil, and disgusting place. It was *literally* disgusting, too, by the way. They never cleaned the place. Instead, they made us do all the dirty work for them.

"Or we have a wonderful state, New Jersey, where you will be taken to attend yet another public high school, which incidentally will also be your last. There, you will be living with a young psychologist, who will talk to you about your problems."

"But… but, you can't do that! I don't have any problems!" Who the hell do these guys think they are? Telling me where I can and can't go? I know I did bad things, but did that seriously mean I had to do all of these?

"Yes, we can," the stupid supervisor spat back. I wanted to punch him right now, but that wouldn't do me any better, seeing as the cops were here with us. "Unless you want to end up somewhere *way worse* than the Orphanage."

Oh, *dammit. Dammit!* There was *no* way out of this one now.

If you enjoyed this sample then look for **The Bad Girl and The Good Boy on Amazon!**

Other books you might enjoy:

Downright Delinquents
Lauren Jackson

Available on Amazon!

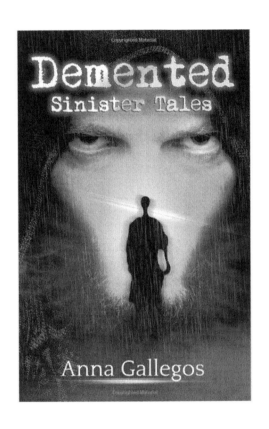

Demented
Anna Gallegos

Available on Amazon!

Introducing the Characters Magazine App

Download the app to get the free issues of interviews from famous fiction characters and find your next favorite book!

iTunes: bit.ly/CharactersApple
Google Play: bit.ly/CharactersAndroid

Acknowledgements

I would like to express my gratitude to the people who provided support, read, offered their comments, and assisted in the editing, proofreading, and design of my book.

I would like to thank BLVNP for enabling me to publish this book.

To my agent Le-an Lacaba, thank you for the assistance and support you bestowed on me despite of your busy schedule.

Thanks to the Wattpad site - for without it, this book would never have found its way to the web and to the people who have been given the opportunity to read it.

Last and certainly not least, to my family and friends who have encouraged me even though it took my time away from them.

Author's Note

Hey there!

Thank you so much for reading Psycho Sitter! I can't express how grateful I am for reading something that was once just a thought inside my head.

I'd love to hear from you! Please feel free to email me at alex-ayers@awesomeauthors.org and sign up at http://alexayers.org/ for freebies!

One last thing: I'd love to hear your thoughts on the book. Please leave a review on Amazon or Goodreads because I just love reading your comments and getting to know YOU!

Whether that review is good or bad, I'd still love to hear it!

Can't wait to hear from you!

Alexandria Ayers

About the Author

Alexandria is a young teenage girl from a small town in Kentucky, who aspires to be a professional writer. Someday she hopes to have her own bookstore.

Her first attempt at writing was on Wattpad, a free site for budding writers. Her book, "Psycho Sitter," received approximately 6 million reads at completion.

Alex enjoys writing and reading fan fiction, as well as, listening to music, where she gets a lot of inspiration for her stories.

22088001R00154

Printed in Great Britain
by Amazon